The Mermaid of Paris

The MERMAID of PARIS

Cary Fagan

KEY PORTER BOOKS

National Library of Canada Cataloguing in Publication Data

Fagan, Cary
       The mermaid of Paris / Cary Fagan.

ISBN 1-55263-232-6

       I. Title.

PS8561.A375M47 2003   C813'.54   C2003-902679-5
PR9199.3.F22M47 2003

THE CANADA COUNCIL | LE CONSEIL DES ARTS
FOR THE ARTS | DU CANADA
SINCE 1957 | DEPUIS 1957

ONTARIO ARTS COUNCIL
CONSEIL DES ARTS DE L'ONTARIO

The publisher gratefully acknowledges the support of the Canada Council
for the Arts and the Ontario Arts Council for its publishing program. We
acknowledge the support of the Government of Ontario through the Ontario
Media Development Corporation's Ontario Book Initiative.

We acknowledge the financial support of the Government of Canada
through the Book Publishing Industry Development Program (BPIDP) for
our publishing activities.

Key Porter Books Limited
70 The Esplanade
Toronto, Ontario
Canada M5E 1R2

www.keyporter.com

Text design: Peter Maher
Electronic formatting: Heidi Palfrey

Printed and bound in Canada

03 04 05 06 07 08 6 5 4 3 2 1

To Jennifer Waring

PART ONE

SPRING 1900

*H*e careened across the lawn in the monocycle of his own invention, a giant iron wheel six feet in diameter, inside which he sat with the spokes surrounding him like the bars of a cage. As he pedalled, a small inner wheel drove the large outer one, sending him across the grass at a speed frightening even to him. He saw as a blur the guests fleeing out of his way and shrieking. Unfortunately, it proved impossible to steer, and he had to concentrate so hard on the action of his feet and maintaining balance that only when it was too late did he see the large red maple directly in his path.

The jarring as the wheel struck the trunk sent shocks through his entire body. The spoke door burst open and he went sprawling backwards onto the grass with the wheel falling half on top of him.

George Beachcroft was the first to reach him. "Are you all right, Henry?" He crouched down to haul the wheel from Henry's legs.

Henry got up and brushed himself off. "Yes, yes, I'm fine." A circle of children in beribboned hats and sailor suits and shining patent shoes had gathered to stare. Henry adjusted his tie and tried to bend his collar back in place. "Where is my hat?"

"Here it is," said one of the boys, handing it to him. Crushed.

"Looks like another one for the shed, Henry," said George Beachcroft.

"I'm afraid so." But he was already distracted, looking for his wife and not seeing her.

The garden sloped gently down to the river, the view of the water prettily obscured by the evenly planted willows. From the lawn the guests had a fine view of the house: terra cotta brick; round, arched, and dormer windows; three chimneys; the sparkling glass panes of the palm house; and the highest point, the turret. A porch veranda swept round the house like a skirt. He liked to see it as if through the eyes of a visitor and then marvel that it was theirs. Their home. If all had been happier he could not possibly have believed in his good fortune. Yet they *were* happy. And had no reason not to be, and perhaps it was just his morbid imagination, or some residual childhood fear.

He organized the children into flying teams, with kites he had made for the day. With only the slightest breeze to hold them aloft, the kites fell back to earth in a series of lowering arcs. But he urged them to keep trying, and they ran like mad across the grass, Henry joining them until he was absolutely winded and had to lean over, hands on his knees, to catch his breath. He could see the ladies admiring the new garden pavilion with its conical roof and rough-hewn benches. The words *rustic* and *delightful* carried across the air. The stiff collar irritated the line between his neck and his jaw, but Meg had laughingly insisted he put it on and he would not have argued with her on such a point. He in turn had watched her, she having sent her maid away, awkwardly prop the heel of her shoe onto the little chair of the dressing table and lean forwards to tie her own laces. The shoe was of the softest kid, and yet when she pulled he saw her grimace painfully. The pains again. But she had only smiled stiffly, pulled harder, and swiftly tied a bow.

She was not on the veranda or in the open doorway.

"Mr. Church." A boy in a sailor suit had come up behind him. "When is the show going to be?"

"Not until after lunch. Why don't you have a go with one of the kites?" He saw George Beachcroft approaching from the garden pavilion, almost as tall as Henry but a good fifty pounds heavier, his beard flourishing where Henry's was closely trimmed. "Church, old fellow," he said, gesturing with the cigar in his hand. "I see that the Missus made you take off the tweeds and corduroys, eh."

"The women keep us civilized, George."

"I suppose, but you've been transformed from inventor to lord of the manor. I was at the other side of the house just now, looking in your birdcages."

"Aviaries."

"Don't be technical with me, Henry. You know I can't understand a thing about these interests of yours. Tell me, though, what's that monstrous large owl you've got? The thing looks like it would tear my throat out with its claws."

"Talons. And it's a great horned. Magnificent, isn't he? You ought to come by some evening and watch him feed. He can drop down on a mouse hidden in the leaves in the blink of an eye."

Several ladies and gentlemen joined them in a casual circle. George's wife, Althea, said, "Mr. Beachcroft, put out that awful-smelling weed. There are ladies present."

"All right, Mrs. Beachcroft." He winked at Henry and dropped the cigar underfoot. But Henry did not smile back, for he steadfastly refused this idea of male comradeship in the face of female oppression. He and Margaret had never lived in such a manner.

"Tell us, Mr. Church," said a woman whose name he could not recall, although her long face and large teeth looked familiar. He could not remember the names of half their acquaintances. "Tell us what birds you can hear now."

"I'm afraid I can't hear anything with the racket those children are making." He smiled apologetically; he did not enjoy being tested like some parlour mesmerist.

"Come on, Henry," said George. "They're much quieter now, dismantling your kites. Do tell us what you hear."

"Yes, do," said Mrs. Rawdon, wife of the manager of the town branch of the Bank of Upper Canada. Henry noticed not her face but her hat, a straw-braid bonnet trimmed with the wing feathers of an osprey. The woman was wearing the remains of a murdered bird on her head and she was asking him what he heard? Yet he did not like to show annoyance and for some reason felt himself flush with embarrassment.

"Come on, old fellow. That's a warbler, isn't it?"

Henry listened; he couldn't prevent himself. "No, a wood thrush. And there's a woodpecker in the oak tree, but don't expect me to tell what kind from the tapping. Chaffinches in the willows. A rose-breasted grosbeak calling to its mate by the trellis. Easy to mistake for a robin, but with more emotion, you might say. Like this—"

He whistled a melodious imitation. The ladies clapped their hands.

"You hear that, Mrs. Beachcroft?" said George. "Whenever I make that whistle I expect you to come running."

"Well, don't you count on it. Not unless you plan to sit on the nest."

Hearty laughter from the men. Henry heard the grosbeak take wing even as he saw Margaret appear in the

13

doorway, shading her eyes to look at the scene upon the lawn. He could have sprinted across the carpet of grass to throw himself at her feet. But he just watched as she lifted the hem of her skirt and came down the veranda steps, already greeting the nearest guests.

The two trestle tables had been laid end to end, draped in Irish linen, and set with the blue picnic porcelain, crystal decanters, silverware reflecting the delirious spring sky. In the centre of each table a Greek urn erupted with hothouse chrysanthemums, roses, daffodils, irises. The adults took their places while the nannies herded the children to their own round tables a good ways off. Down the veranda steps came the row of servants with trays of watercress salad, cold leek soup, roast shoulder of lamb, devilled kidneys, veal pie, pickled mushrooms.

George Beachcroft was saying, "Remember that contraption you built, Henry, the shower bath where you had to pedal to operate the pump that sprayed the water over your head? That was last year, wasn't it? You demonstrated in a bathing costume and Mrs. DeVries was quite scandalized. Another brilliant idea that was too clever for the marketplace."

"No, that was two years ago," Henry said, but he was only half listening. He sat at one end of the tables, Margaret at the other. He admired how she kept the conversation at her end so lively. On social occasions he found himself either wordless or running breathlessly on about some latest notion until he noticed the look of tedious boredom on his listeners' faces. Well, they found him amusing and dull both, he knew, a performing fool.

Mrs. Beachcroft leaned close and spoke softly, not to exclude those around them from hearing but out of sympathy for her subject. "I am so glad to see Margaret without the arm band. It is time."

"Yes, time," he said.

"Those damn Boers are worse than the African savages they live among," said Mr. Wiffing, shaking his spectacles at them.

"I approve of the sentiment if not the language, Mr. Wiffing," said Mrs. Beachcroft. "And now with those poor boys in Nafking—"

"I tell Mrs. Beachcroft that she ought to read only the ladies' pages of the newspaper," said George. The edge of his moustache and beard was whitened from the asparagus cream sauce. "It does her no good."

"You think that we cannot comprehend the intricacies of war, Mr. Beachcroft?" said Mrs. Henshaw.

"On the contrary, you understand too well. I am afraid that you will become our generals and the next conflict will be even bloodier."

His harrumph of laughter obviously irritated his wife, but George didn't care the way Henry would have. Perhaps he ought to be more like George. "What tosh," Mrs. Beachcroft said. "Women would not send their sons to war at all. And he was such a sweet young man, our dear Margaret's brother. How she doted on him. They had a special bond, the two of them, a rare sympathy and understanding. And of course their father expected so much from him. He would have—oh well, it's no matter now."

He knew that she was right and that Margaret had not been the same in the last months since Alasdair had been killed. She was more withdrawn and alone. Alasdair had been a truly good fellow, supportive of Henry during his courtship of Margaret. He turned to his wife's friend. "You are only right, Mrs. Beachcroft. Alasdair would have held my present position in the company. I have no doubt that he would have excelled in it far beyond my own managerial abilities."

"He chose to honour the Queen instead," said Mrs. Netherton, who still wore mourning after seventeen years, in imitation of the ailing Victoria.

"Plain foolish if you ask me," said Mr. Wiffing. "He had a responsibility to the business that his father built with his own ingenuity and labour. That is why a new form of government, fully independent of England—"

"Oh, you mustn't, Mr. Wiffing," said Mrs. Wiffing, who had turned away from the conversation in the middle of the table. "Do not begin your speeches about a Canadian republic and the glories of the country to the south. Before dessert you will be on to annexation. From all accounts, Mr. Church, you are doing splendidly at the company. But poor Mrs. Church. Your beautiful wife was so very close to her older brother, especially after they lost their mother in that terrible storm."

"Yes," Henry said solemnly. He did not want to speak of Margaret; he was almost too vividly aware of her presence at the other end of the tables. They expected more from him, but he could find nothing in himself to offer. A boy of five or six ran up to their end of the table. His white shoes and stockings had been muddied by going down to the edge of the river.

"Mr. Church," the boy said breathlessly. "We are all waiting."

He was glad to be rescued. "Are you?"

"Yes, we've finished our cake and ices and want to see the show."

"What a cheeky boy you are," Mrs. Beachcroft said.

The boy looked down and then threw himself at Mrs. Beachcroft, who was his mother, and buried his face in her lap. She stroked and kissed him.

"When are you going to cut that boy's curls?" said Mr. Wiffing.

"My little Sampson? Never!"

From the children's tables rose a ragged chant accompanied by the banging of spoons.

"Savages," said Mr. Wiffing. "Worse than the Boers. You better satisfy their primitive needs, Henry, before they demonstrate their cannibal desires."

"I'm sure it must seem very foolish."

"Oh, but the children love it so," Mrs. Henshaw said.

He wiped his mouth with a napkin. "If Mrs. Church doesn't mind."

As he rose he tried to catch his wife's eye. She was speaking with animation and waving her slim hand. At that moment she knocked over a water glass, soaking the bosom of her dress. She cried out, pressing her hands against the wet material as if to feel that she had really done it. Only then did she look up, see Henry, and smile at him with her eyes.

She once whispered that she loved him for retaining a boy's heart. Now he felt self-conscious of her watching while he fussed about the stage, concocted from a farmhouse table and a taffeta curtain. In front, the children tussled over their places on the veranda steps. Most of the adults stood on the grass nearby or up on the veranda itself, the women in wicker chairs and the men leaning on the rail. And she, Margaret, at the very edge of the frame of his vision.

He blew furiously on a toy trumpet and with the other hand jerkily pulled back the curtain. Then turned his back a moment and came round again with a marionette some three feet tall, a clown in a striped outfit and drooping hat and a tremendous carved nose like Punch. The clown held a stack of three balls on one of its oversized hands, which it seemed to be examining, head cocked to one side.

The marionette looked up. "What? Who's out there?" A ridiculous squeaking voice, so much more forceful than his own.

Shouts from the children.

"Children, is it? Demanding, ill-behaved, difficult, dastardly children?"

Shouts of "No, we aren't" and the like.

"And I suppose you wish to be entertained? I suppose you wish to see me juggle these three balls?"

Affirmative cries.

"All right, then, if I must. I will perform some astonishing feats of juggling never before attempted by a creature made of wood and stuffing. And then we will see another incident in the adventures of Mr. Pickwick. It is entitled 'Mr. Pickwick Climbs a Wall.'"

"Pickwick! Pickwick!"

"Now, are you ready? One ... two ... three ..."

The clown tossed his hand and the three balls made a slow arc in the air, coming down one at a time on his nose.

"Oh! Ow! Ee!"

Great laughing and clapping.

He risked a glance towards her. She had an enigmatic smile, as if painted by da Vinci, whose sketchbooks he venerated. And now Althea Beachcroft came up to lay her hand on Margaret's arm.

He yanked the curtain closed, hastily arranged the props. And then opened the curtain again, to Sam Weller trying to hoist Mr. Pickwick over the papier-mâché wall. The children's laughter tumbled over the lawn.

In the evening she suffered another painful episode. He kept by her side as she lay on the bed, the pains rising up her legs as if long needles, heated to burning, were pushing up through the soles of her feet. So she had described it to him after the last one; now she could not speak. From the bowl of cold water he drew a cloth, wrung out the excess water, then placed it against her skin, the hem of her nightgown drawn up. Another compress and a third, from her ankles up to her thighs, while she arched her back and, shuddering, whimpered through clenched teeth.

"Please, Meg, let me call Doctor Walsh. He will help you."

"No."

Her mouth moved but no further words came out. Last time the doctor had given her a solution of four percent cocaine; the pain subsided but she had revolted at the effects. He took her hand, and her trembling fingers tried to press against his. She jolted upright with sudden force, doubling over and moaning in an inhuman manner. It took him some moments before he could gently ease her down again. His love, his dear love so cruelly treated. If he could only take on her pain. He would do anything to help her.

He had fallen asleep at his desk in the turret study, the sketches beneath his cheek dampened by his breath. He sat up and stretched out the ache in his shoulders, looking out of the three curving windows to see that it was still night. The middle window had been left open, and cold air washed over him. A full moon, low and white and huge over the river, turned the water to a black luminescence and the willow trees to silver, their moving leaves making a sound like sand shifting in a pan.

One of the birds trilled in the aviary. He remembered something that he had read in the newspaper just this morning, that Vesuvius was erupting in southern Italy. Molten lava pouring down its side while ash darkened the air just as it had in Roman times when Pompeii and Herculaneum had been blanketed into death. Civilizations destroyed by the power of nature. We lived in an age of hubris, of human achievement previously unknown, mimicking nature with our steam engines and electrical generators, but there were still forces we did not understand and could not control.

He went downstairs to check on Margaret, whose torment had finally subsided, allowing her to sleep. He walked on tiptoe so as not to wake her. But when he looked into the room the bed was empty. A breeze billowed the curtains. So confused was he at not seeing Margaret in bed that he went over and lifted the sheets, then looked behind it in case she had somehow fallen. He went back into the hall and would have checked the lavatory if he had not heard a sound—the muffled yet distinct thump of the front door closing. He bounded down the hall to the main staircase and jumped half the steps to reach the vestibule.

And here she was, not only standing in her robe, but drying her dripping hair with a towel.

"Margaret! What is going on?"

"I didn't think you were awake. I went for a swim."

"Now? In the river? With your condition? I don't understand."

"It's all right, Henry, really. It helped my pains immensely, just as I thought it might. And it felt so lovely. You know how much I love the water. See, I'm myself again." She laughed and took his arm. "Come and let's creep into the kitchen and make a cup of tea. We must be careful not to wake up Mrs. Hendricks or she'll give us a scolding."

"I cannot believe my eyes. You should go back to bed, Margaret. I must insist upon it."

"I couldn't possibly sleep now. Are you coming or not?" She dropped his arm in a pretend huff and started down the hall.

"Well, of course," he said, catching up. They had kept their voices low, as if the servants really might punish them if they were caught. Henry followed her into the back of the house and through the heavy kitchen door. In the gloom the copper pans gleamed from the brick wall above the double sink. The long table where the servants ate their meals was already set for their early morning breakfast. He watched her bend down before the range and open the door of the firebox. "There are still some warm coals," she said. She used the scoop in the coal bucket to feed in more, banged about with the poker, and then closed the door again and put the kettle on.

"Are you not cold?" he asked, coming up to her and touching her wet hair. The shoulders of her robe were damp. "For you to catch a chill now could be very dangerous."

"Oh, please don't fuss, Henry," she said, her eyes shining. "It's so pleasing to do something out of the ordinary for a change. Don't you feel that?"

He wasn't sure that he did, but he had no wish to contradict her. Having grown up as an orphan, he had tried only to learn what was the proper and expected thing. And even in that he had often felt his failings. She stopped his thoughts by kissing him, allowing her mouth to open so that he felt the warm tip of her tongue. His arousal was immediate.

"Oh, Margaret."

"Don't you 'Oh, Margaret' me," she said with a little laugh and then kissed him again, deeply this time. Her hand moved up the inside of his leg, making him catch his breath. He pressed against her, feeling the shape of her through her robe which she was already pulling open. He wanted no will of his own. He was all hers.

The factory was seven miles down the road, three miles past the other side of the town. In the previous week he had ridden there on his new prototype, a foot-and-hand-propelled bicycle in which the rider not only pedalled but also pumped the two long handlebars that were connected by jointed metal bars to the pedals themselves. But the additional speed and ease of riding had not materialized. In fact, the machine had turned out to be more tiring to ride rather than less, causing a strain in the shoulder and back muscles, and the action of the hands had only interfered with the efficient rotation of the pedals.

And so today he left it in the shed with the other discards and rode to work on his Dawes Country Speed model instead, the knees of his long legs rising and falling, his suit jacket flapping in the wind, his hat pressed firmly onto his head. While he had made a dozen improvements in the Dawes bicycles, they had until now been minor—in the hubs, the brakes, the chain, and the seat suspension. And most of those changes had appeared almost simultaneously on bicycles from other companies. He had not yet made a great breakthrough, something revolutionary. It was such a simple and handsome thing, the workings of the bicycle in its present form, and the improvements of the last fifteen years—wheels of the same size, pneumatic tires, socket steering—had only enhanced that simplicity. His own ideas tended to complicate things.

This morning he and James had fed the birds, an activity during which new ideas sometimes came to him. But today, nothing. The breeding pair of ring-necked pheasants and the mourning doves flew towards his tin bucket of seed, while the wrens and thrushes and vireos hopped excitedly about the branches. In the traps they had caught seven mice, enough for the night feeding of the owls, the kestrel, and the goshawk. After he was done he had stood for some time watching the beautiful mechanics of them, the combination of lightness, strength, and aeronautical engineering that allowed them to take flight. That was what really interested him—not their social or nesting habits, but the structural differences of their bodies that made one manoeuvrable, another superb at gliding in wind currents, a third quick, a fourth powerful over long distances. Perhaps what a bicycle really needed was wings.

He arrived at the factory as the men were filing in under the wrought-iron sign over the gate. *Dawes Bicycle Manufactury*. It struck him each morning as a miniature kingdom of its own, with its army of citizens marching into place and his father-in-law as all-powerful ruler. They touched their caps to Henry as they headed into one of the three yellow-brick buildings, each connected to the others by an enclosed bridge. A private railway siding came up from the main track for the trains bringing in materials and taking out the finished bicycles to dealers across the country. And, just to the north, the narrow workers' houses, the play yard for the children, the company store, and the community house for what Mr. Dawes called "healthful amusements." The men who stoked the boilers and ran the engines had arrived in the dark hours so that the power was waiting for the forges, the punch and drill presses, the sprocket machines, the gang saws and rivetting machines, the electrochemical plating works, the millers, brazing stands, enamelling ovens, sandblast plant. Henry dusted himself off and walked into Building One as the whistle sounded and the roar and grind of labour began.

Each building had its own assistant foreman, with MacMurtrie, the head foreman, overseeing them all, but still Henry walked through each floor to see that the assembly route was running efficiently so that it would not get backed up and leave other departments idle. The men truing frames said, "Good morning, Boss," a form of address that he did not enjoy and that sounded to him unintentionally ironic. He was not, despite his father-in-law's hopes, a good manager. He had no talent for supervising other men, ensuring the honesty of suppliers, docking pay, and invoking other forms of discipline. As a result, he was sure the men did not respect him. The truth known even to himself was that he had risen above his station.

The men were almost all foreign-born Irish and English or else Poles, Russians, and Italians. The newest employee, a young Italian fellow with rather romantic features, was opening the high windows by means of the chain-link pulleys. It was the Italians who had pooled together the money for the Edison phonograph with an extra-large horn and which was even now playing *La Traviata* beneath the sound of hammering. As he toured the floor he was conscious of the men surreptitiously watching his movements and expressions. And so he acted the role, hefting a frame and eyeing it for trueness, examining the welds between the tubes for any weakness caused by removal of the spelter. He counted the finished frames from the evening before and then strode purposely over to Giancarlo Caporale, the head of the department, who, no doubt expecting him, put down his hammer and took out a large handkerchief to wipe his brow. Like the other men, he wore a white shirt with the sleeves rolled, a stiff black hat, cotton trousers. His face was slate grey and his receding hair had left a lone tuft on his forehead so that the other Italians called him *il caprone*, the goat.

Henry said, "Why did you fall behind yesterday?"

"The bottom bracket. A crack. I send over a hundred back. A big argument with the braziers. Mr. Dawes, he come down and agree with me. Now is fixed."

A silent criticism of himself, perhaps. He ought not to have left early to work at home on his idea for a bicycle fan. Fixed over a rider's head, it was supposed to work by the action of the rotating front wheel to cool the rider as he travelled. "I see. And when will you catch up?"

"By noon."

"All right."

"Boss, you have a chance maybe to read that matter we spoke of?"

For a moment he considered how to answer. Then he reached into his jacket and from the pocket drew a small booklet. "I think it is unwise to give such things to the man who governs your employment."

"But I am giving it as a matter of intellectual interest." He ran his hand over the tuft of hair. "Because you are a man of science, of enlightenment, not burdened by the chains of religion."

"But I don't agree with this Malatesta any more than the others. It makes no sense to me. A society cannot exist without authority."

"Only because we do not respect ourselves as individuals. If each of us listens to our own authority, to our own hearts, then we will be as a society of princes. We cannot be our noble selves without freedom."

"It is duty, not freedom, that makes us noble, Giancarlo."

"If each of us is truly free, then each of us truly knows our duty. To others and to ourselves. What is this life for, Mr. Church? In Italy I am a glove maker and at least I can take pride in my work. Yes, I am poor, but I make excellent gloves and I know the name of every woman who wears them. And then machines come and take away the work of our hands and so I come here. Now I am part of that machine that takes away my dignity. And it is a shame because a bicycle, well, a bicycle is an anarchist invention at heart, I think. But still, in some small way I remain free. It is the bosses, I think, who are most unfree. We who work here are afraid of losing our jobs, yes. But the bosses, they have deeper fears."

"I don't know what you are talking about."

"Because you cannot own another soul."

"I don't wish to."

"No, but you are forced to."

"Giancarlo, I don't know what you expect to accomplish. I read what you give me but I don't recognize what I know of mankind in these works. I don't recognize myself. Humans are weak. They need government, laws, conventions, the social structure that keeps us decent and civilized. We could not live without them."

"But that is also fear."

"And what sort of fear is this now?"

"The fear of being free. Just like those birds that you keep as prisoners in their cages."

"They are better off than if they lived in the wild. They eat every day. They are protected from predators."

"Yes, but what is the price? Their freedom, their right to live as true birds. And what happens if you leave the cage doors open? Will the birds fly out?"

"That is a curious question. I haven't thought about it."

"I believe they do not. The cage has become their world. They grow too fond of their enslavement and are afraid to leave it and become real birds again. No longer are they being responsible for their existence. No, the birds do not leave their cages. They wait for someone to close the doors again so that they can feel safe."

"You are being too clever. We are hardly birds."

"No, our situation is different because we have to remove our own shackles, and that is even more difficult to do. Yes, there is always fear. Of our true selves."

"Enough, Giancarlo. I don't know how you expect to convince me when you can't even persuade your fellow workers."

"Oh, there are some anarchists among us even in this one department. Not most, no. But some here, and many more back in Italy and in France and Russia."

"Yes, throwing bombs and assassinating royalty."

Giancarlo's face grew stern. "This is not what I believe in. These are a few only, angry men, lonely, with voices haunting them. Tragic figures. But here, I have something else for you." He took a small book from his pocket and handed it casually to Henry. "By Proudhon. You know him? I believe you read in French. Perhaps this book is making more of an impression."

Henry put the book in his pocket. "I read French only with difficulty. And what if it does make an impression? What would you like me to do? Read it to my birds?"

Giancarlo did not even smile; he was looking behind and above Henry's shoulder. Henry turned to see his father-in-law at the second-floor office window from which he could see all the factory departments below. He was leaning heavily on his two canes, looking down on them.

Henry said, "I think Mr. Dawes would prefer to see us both at our tasks."

"Yes, Boss."

"I want a note sent to me when the work is caught up. And the name of the man responsible for the bad frames."

"Ah, that we never did find out."
Henry saw Giancarlo smile.

A letter from Chester Canty:

Even Edison did not allow his thinking to go as far as it might.
You need stimulation, competition, and the sharing of ideas.
If you come to one of our meetings in Toronto you will get all
of that and more. After my own day at the bank, I find it a tonic.
All right, you will hear some old windbags too, like Macpherson,
who can't stop talking about his alternating-current shoe-
polishing machine. Or Strickland, with his hat conformator. But
ideas need nourishment, and you are starving in the wilderness...

He looked through the turret window, from which
he could see only dark lawn, the outlines of trees, and
the black space he knew was the river. During the day the
spires of the Anglican and Catholic churches were visible
and, farther east, the tallest smokestack of the Dawes factory, but it had all vanished. Chester was right, he ought
to go to Toronto for a few days, but he could not get himself to leave Margaret, who did not care for cities. Even so,
he was feeling almost desperate to make a name for himself; today alone he had sketched three new inventions,
each more ridiculous than the last. All of them involved
motors of some sort, even though his real interest was in
the efficient use of human energy. No doubt it was egotis-
tical of him to consider such inventions more artistic. Or
perhaps he simply felt the limitations, the restrictions of
being human.

"Henry, will you come downstairs?"

He turned in his chair to see Margaret standing in the doorway at the top of the turret stairs. She had let her hair down to her shoulders. So caught up in his own thoughts had he been that she was like an apparition. He started to stutter something.

She said, "I'll have Cook make us something warm to drink," and went down again.

The night had turned cool, and a small fire burned in the back parlour, which they did not use for company. The only other light came from a gas lamp with a frosted tulip glass cover on the end table by the divan on which she reclined. Henry looked at the small books on the mantel.

"What shall it be?" he said. "Wordsworth? Arnold, perhaps."

"As you wish."

"Oh, but I forgot for a moment that you can't abide either of them. Too simple-minded, you said."

"It is not that. They write too much of themselves and their deep feelings. I find it tiresome. But you didn't forget and are teasing me. I really don't mind if you choose something to your own taste tonight."

"I am reading to you, Meg, and must choose in order to please. You prefer a more intellectual poet. You are far brighter than I am."

"Now you are humouring me, which I don't like."

"No, it's true. I don't have ideas, except for how one gear may drive another. How about Keats as a compromise?"

She lowered her head. "Not this evening."

He felt himself colour. "I am sorry, Margaret. I forgot that Keats had been Alasdair's favourite."

"Yes."

"I wish that I could somehow compensate for the loss of him. Be more to you, Meg."

She stared into the fire. "You are so well-meaning, Henry. A sibling remembers who you were as a child. Knows the house you grew up in. Loved the same father and mother. We weren't alike. Alasdair took after my father—that is, my father as a young man. I am my mother's child. Alasdair knew me and accepted me, more easily than I do myself. He was the one person who understood." She looked at Henry and pretended to smile. "That's all it is. My childhood companion is gone. Now, are you going to read or not?"

"I am. And I think it must be Mr. Browning."

"Yes, please. And if you don't mind, I shall be most improper and take off my shoes."

"The pains again? Allow me."

She tried to pull her feet away, but he knelt and began to unlace her shoe. He pulled it off gently, letting his hand slip down her ankle to her heel. Then the other.

"When are you going to speak to Doctor Walsh? Perhaps he will have a different treatment."

"The doctor will just say that I have one of those mysterious women's ailments."

"You must get better, Margaret, if we are to take that walking tour of Italy. You have never been abroad." He got up, brushing off the knees of his trousers. "Let me find something I don't know. I shall stand by the mantel with the fire beside me and be a very picture for you. Ah, here's one.

'Any Wife to Any Husband.' I suppose you ought to be reading it to me."

"But I prefer to listen."

He read in an unadorned voice, merely pausing at the end of each line and verse.

But now, because the hour through years was fixed,
Because our inmost beings met and mixed,
Because thou once hast loved me—wilt thou dare
Say to thy soul and Who may list beside,
"Therefore she is immortally my bride;
Chance cannot change that love, nor time impair..."

He read for several minutes. He put the book on the mantel and could not prevent himself from falling to his knees before her, burying his face in her lap.

"Meg, Meg."

He kissed the folds of her dress and felt her hand stroke his hair. His own hands caressed her legs through the material of her gown and he pressed kisses against her, moving until he kissed her *there* and she moved in such a way he knew she felt the sweet pressure. But then he pulled back and looked up at her in supplication.

"I love you most dearly, Meg. I am grateful to be your husband."

"You do not need to feel that way." She stood up.

"What is it, Meg? Have I offended you?"

She moved around him and walked quickly from the room, down the hall to the back staircase. He went after her but was fearful of catching up, running only so that he might take hold of the door of her dressing room as it was swinging shut. He could but watch as she clutched the sides of the wash basin, her shoulders shaking violently. He wanted to put his hands on her but instead he poured her a glass of water and she took it from him with a trembling hand.

"Please, Margaret, tell me what is the matter."

"I am so hideous. Do not say kind things to me. Now please let me be alone."

He obeyed, closing the door behind him.

He drove the carriage himself and left it with the stable boy at the gate. Before him rose the great house of Jeremiah Dawes, the stone entrance set in the terra cotta walls, arched windows alternating with rectangular porticoes and columns, and five peaks to the slate roof. The gardener was wheeling a load of mulch around the glasshouse.

His father-in-law was the only man in the district to keep a butler, who now showed Henry to the library. Mr. Dawes was sunk into a leather armchair behind the desk as if he had become a part of the chair itself, the way a tree will grow around and finally fuse with some obstruction such as a fence post. The curtains remained closed—Mr. Dawes could no longer tolerate the sun—and the only light came from a green-shaded lamp on the desk. Henry felt the usual apprehension rise in him, just as it had when he was a boy at the orphanage and Mr. Dawes had become his benefactor.

"Sit down, Henry."

"Thank you, sir."

He took one of the medieval-style armchairs facing the desk and perched uncomfortably on the brass-studded edge so as to appear attentive.

"All right, Henry. You tell me what we are to do."

"For the short term, I think we have no choice but to ask the bank to have our line of credit raised."

"And the interest?"

"I cannot say for certain, but I will try to limit it to an increase of one-quarter percent."

"Usury." Slowly he placed the tips of his fingers together on the desk before him. "And can you account for it?"

"Account, sir?"

"For the plummet. The plummet in sales."

"It is universal. All the manufacturers are suffering. The fashion for bicycles has slowed. It is worse in Britain and the United States."

"And if our sales keep dropping?"

"I hope they will not."

"That is hardly an answer. We must begin to cut costs. Reduce our inventory. At the same time we must strive for a larger percentage of the marketplace. Advertising. Promotion. Lower prices. Listen to me carefully, Henry. I have struggled to survive as a manufacturer for twenty years. Organs and pianos, bathroom fixtures, farm implements. Only with bicycles did I finally achieve genuine success. I do not plan to live just long enough to see the company that I founded and that grew to prominence on my sacrifice and perseverance descend into bankruptcy. I accepted you as a son-in-law without a penny to your name because you were bright and hard-working and had no expectations of your own. I did not anticipate that you would lack all passion for success. Well, it is about time you acquired what you lack, Henry. I will not see the Dawes Bicycle Manufactury fail. And I will not see my only daughter living in reduced circumstances. Do you understand me?"

"Of course, sir."

His father-in-law shifted his lower jaw back and forth, as if unable to find a resting place without discomfort. Henry was as concerned as his father-in-law, only he did not feel confident of his ability to reverse the company's decline. But he must succeed, if only for Margaret's sake.

"Speaking of my daughter," said Mr. Dawes, "I wish to have one last word. You have been married five years and I have no grandchildren."

"I mean no disrespect, sir, if I say that is a subject between Margaret and myself."

"I believe I have a right. Doctor Walsh tells me that neither you nor Margaret has consulted him on this matter. My son was taken from me, and all my hopes reside with the two of you. I am not well. It is not asking too much to see my own grandchild, or at least to know of the expectation of one, before I die. For what reason have I worked all these years? Why have I lived alone, without Margaret's mother, whom I adored and without whom life has seemed without purpose? I have a right, I believe I have a right."

They fell into silence, the two men surrounded by their own gloom. Henry could hear his father-in-law's laboured breathing. The chandelier gently tinkled from some heavy movement on the floor above, a cabinet being shifted or a bed replaced by the servants. Henry said, "There is something that I have wanted to ask you about, sir."

"Go on."

"It is also a difficult subject, as it refers to the tragic event in your own life, sir. About the ship. The *Jewel of Breton*."

"I see."

"Margaret herself has never spoken of it to me, and yet I feel that it has had great subsequent consequences for her. I hesitate to intrude on your sorrow, but it is Margaret I wish to understand."

His father-in-law drew his fingers away from one another. He seemed to be thinking; perhaps he realized that the question was in part an answer to his own inquiry. "Yes," he said at last. "I will tell you what I know. Margaret was just a girl of nine. She and Mrs. Dawes had gone to visit relations in Halifax. There was a wedding—an unusual time of year, but the bride, Mrs. Dawes' sister, was almost thirty and once the engagement was made there was a desire not to delay until the following summer. My wife had not seen her family since before our marriage, and I had given them permission to go, only asking for my son to stay behind. Mrs. Dawes' letters had been very cheerful, as she was glad to be among her own people. Indeed, they were having such a pleasant time that my wife asked if she and Margaret might delay their return home and visit her cousins who were just returning to New York. I was reluctant."

"Because of the season," Henry said.

"Even along the coast the sea becomes more rough as winter approaches. But I checked with our own shipping company and as the waters were still reasonably calm I agreed. Mrs. Dawes and Margaret boarded the *Jewel of Breton* and were to sail down the coast to Long Island, stay two weeks, and travel home by train and coach. But they did not get farther than the coast of Maine. There was a storm."

"I understand it was some unusual weather occurrence."

"An ice floe had broken up near Newfoundland. But the ice shards were still large, some the size of a carriage. They were moving south, away from shore, but then the storm arose and by some confluence of winds drew the ship among them. The sea was rough and rain lashed down and then the ship and the ice collided in the darkness. The collisions shook the hull until one punched through the port side. It began taking in water very fast."

"And where were Mrs. Dawes and Margaret?"

"I believe they were in their cabin. Knowing my wife, she would have been determined only to protect her child. At some point she must have decided to go up onto the deck. That in itself must have been a trial. By all reports the ship was already listing badly and it was almost impossible to stand upright in the wind and rain. They would have had to crawl to the side where the life vessels were being lowered. There was only one left and it was already full. Mrs. Dawes managed to get Margaret into it."

"She remained on ship?"

"There was no room for her."

"What unspeakable horror."

"I have been told that she was very calm, almost as if she did not feel any danger for herself."

Mr. Dawes reached out for a glass of water on the desk. His hand was slow to move it to his lips. Impatient to know more, Henry asked, "And did Margaret remain in the lifeboat until it reached shore?"

"I wish that were so. Another passenger, a man who had jumped ship, encountered the lifeboat in the water. He climbed over the side and, in order to make room for himself, he—he threw Margaret out."

37

"That cannot be!"

"Of course, that is not what he said afterwards. He insisted to the authorities that she fell. But I have made my own inquiries among the other witnesses. She was sacrificed."

"Monstrous. And yet she survived. Was she picked up by another boat?"

"I do not know how she reached the shore. The survivors weathered the storm until daybreak, when they were towed in by the local fishermen. Margaret was not on any boat, yet she was found wandering on the beach among the others. How she got there no one was able to say, and Margaret either could not remember or would not tell me."

Henry found he could say nothing. The suffering of his own Margaret, who had been so young, was too much even to imagine.

"I hope that she really has forgotten," Mr. Dawes said. "That would be a blessing."

Henry tried to find his own voice. "I knew that she must have spent time in the water. Doctor Walsh believes that extreme cold may have caused some nerve damage to her legs. That is why she suffers such pain."

Now it was Mr. Dawes' turn to be silent. Again he reached for the water glass, only this time his fingers tipped it over. The water spilled as the glass rolled off the edge of the table to the carpet. Henry pulled out his handkerchief.

"No, leave it. Just send in the maid as you go out. It is time for me to rest."

He had been dismissed. Replacing his handkerchief, he stepped over the glass and walked out of the room.

On the steps of the bank he adjusted his tie and let himself breathe a moment. The meeting with Rawdon, the bank manager, had not gone as well as he had hoped. The credit line had been increased, but only on agreement of a half-percent rise in interest. His father-in-law would not be pleased.

He began to walk along the main street, the sidewalks a bustle of women doing their shopping and boys dodging between the horses tied in front of the farm supply depot. He was regretting the need to go back to the factory for the rest of the afternoon when a tapping on the window next to him made him stop and turn.

There was Althea Beachcroft, knocking her ring on the glass inside Castle's Tea Shop. She was sitting with his own Margaret at the table by the front window, his wife smiling wanly at him. He tipped his hat and went in, the little bell jangling on the door. It was a woman's place, all pink curtains and lace, tins of tea decorated with Ceylonese plantation scenes lining the open shelves above the wainscotting. Between the women sat a pot of tea, another of hot water, and a dish of sweets.

"Mr. Church, would you like to join us? I was just telling our dear Margaret that she does not have enough interests."

"Please don't go on about it," Margaret said. Her eyes looked red; had she been crying?

"But Mrs. Beachcroft is right," said Henry, more earnestly than he intended. He did not sit down, feeling that he had interrupted, yet it was awkward to stand above them.

"Althea has enough interests for the both of us." And she tried to laugh.

"Eating all the jam tarts, for one," said Althea. "But I am not making a joke, my dear. The little things in life are what give us pleasure. A new pair of gloves. A garden party that is declared a success. One's husband's accomplishments. Our own accomplishments."

"You have so many, Althea. Your charitable work. Your beautiful children."

"What you need is an enthusiasm, Margaret. Don't you agree, Mr. Church? Something to get Margaret out of her stubborn sulks. Why don't you come with me and join the Women's Conversation and Bicycling Society? Really, Margaret. Your own father and husband make bicycles and you don't even ride one. I tell you it is the greatest lark. Every Saturday we take over the roads. You can't imagine what an exhilarating sensation it is to go soaring down a hill on a bicycle. The wind in your face, feet pedalling like mad. It's sheer ecstasy. George says I love my bicycle more than I love him, and I'm afraid he may be right."

They all laughed. Henry's face felt flushed. Margaret picked up her teacup and wrapped her hands around it, but did not drink. "Henry has tried to get me on one of those things, but I just feel no interest in it. Perhaps it's those bloomers you wear. They look so—"

"Ridiculous? I admit they don't exactly flatter the figure—at least not my figure. But you can't always be a Gibson girl, my dear."

"I'm not!"

"Mr. Church, if your wife will not find an interest in something, then we will have to provide one for her. Don't you agree?"

"Oh yes, quite."

"I have it. You shall redecorate your large parlour."

"But what is wrong with it?"

"Nothing at all. That isn't the point. Bring it up to the latest fashion. You could completely do it over *à la Japonaise*. How chic it would look!"

"I don't know that I care enough to bother."

"Nonsense. I insist that you do it. We will start looking for patterns this afternoon. And if you make one peep about the expense, Mr. Church—"

"But I am only too glad if it will give Margaret pleasure."

"You see that, Margaret? You are undeservedly spoiled. Now go away, Mr. Church, we have important decorating matters to discuss. And you pour me another cup of tea, Margaret. I'm as thirsty as an Israelite in the desert today."

He considered it a privilege to watch her brush out her long hair at the dressing table, which she did while softly humming. He did not want to disturb the moment, which felt so natural and ordinary, as if everything was right in the world, but on the other hand he wanted to hear her speak and so he said, "What is that melody you always hum?"

"My nanny taught it to me," she said, without pausing. "Madame Delaire. She was very fragile-looking, with skin so translucent that thin veins showed in her nose. But something happened and she was dismissed along with the valet. No one ever talked about it, and to me it was a great mystery and very exciting. After her came Madame Guillot, a widow. Not attractive, but with lustrous dark hair that she brushed a hundred strokes every evening. She used to make

me count aloud, I remember. '*Quarante et un, quarante-deux . . .*'
And now I always count in French, I can't help it."

She went back to humming. Her spirits had been better
the last few days; perhaps Althea Beachcroft had been right.
It was all so simple. He felt almost light-headed.

As he came down the hall he could hear her talking to
the wallpaper hanger, a red-haired, broad-shouldered fellow with a nose flattened as if from a fall or fisticuffs.
They had brought him in from Toronto, as Althea had
insisted the ones in town weren't good enough, and the
paper hanger had pitched his tent at the end of the lawn
by the river.

Henry did not like changes in his surroundings. But the
carpet had been taken up, the walls stripped, the light
sconces removed. Yesterday the rolls of wallpaper had
arrived, an intricate pattern of crossed bamboo stalks and
lilies, made by the Halcyon Company of Winetka, Illinois.
Margaret had unrolled it for him hesitantly, unsure of her
own taste, and so he had overpraised it, which had resulted
in the opposite of its intended effect.

He stopped just outside the doorway. The two in the
room had stopped talking and now a whistling began.
Margaret must have been watching the fellow at work.

"What is that song you are whistling?" Margaret's voice.
The impropriety of eavesdropping, but he could not resist.

"You never heard it, ma'am? It's called 'I'll Meet You
Under the Moon' and it's very popular just now. They sang
it down at the Horse's Mouth last night.

"The Horse's Mouth. Is that a tavern?"

"Just outside of town. But it's not a disreputable watering hole of plotting and licentiousness. It's very convivial. I was meaning to ask you, ma'am, what you were wanting to do about the inglenook. I mean whether I ought to run the wallpaper right to the flagstones or not."

"I haven't thought about it. What do you think?"

"I never yet been hired for my opinion, ma'am, but I think running it right up would look very cozy. And if you don't mind me saying so, ma'am, and meaning no disrespect, I think you would make a very pretty sight sitting here on a winter's night."

"Please finish the room."

Her voice was suddenly curt. Henry, like a schoolboy about to be caught, hurried down the hall.

A dozen or so children marched along the road from town, making enough noise to bring out several of the household staff, among them Mrs. Hendricks, the cook; James, the master's valet; and Mary, the mistress's maid. Henry himself had not been home long from the office. Having just changed his clothes, he came down the veranda stairs, polishing his watch with his handkerchief and then slipping it back into his vest pocket.

"And what's this about?" he said.

"The rascal won't tell us," said James, scowling at the boy in the front, who was struggling to hold up a wooden box marked "Pinkham's Regularity Drops." He wore a pair of knee pants and mended stockings and a dirty yellow jacket with the sleeves rolled up. The others kept pushing him from behind and he half turned to mutter threats at them.

Henry crouched down to him. "What's your name, young man?"

"George Tilset, sir."

"Who's your father, George?"

"Alfred Tilset, sir, as works at present in the quarry."

"And you've brought something for me."

"Yes, sir. Found it in the alley behind the post office. They was going to murder it, so we snatched it and brought it to you."

"That's well done. Let's have a look."

"He's likely to take off your finger, sir."

"Then we better be careful. Perhaps you should put the box on the ground."

Relieved, the boy half dropped it. The other children pressed around, with the staff leaning over them from behind. Henry grasped the lid with his large hands and lifted it quickly. The black thing inside lunged for his hand but he drew clear of its reach and it shrank back again.

"Mercy, Mr. Church," said Mary. "So big already, but it looks like a baby. What sort of bird is it?"

"A raven. *Corvus corax principalis*."

"He looks fierce as the devil."

"Just frightened." Henry examined the pinfeathers bristling on the head, the clear eyes, ebony beak. The bird tilted its head to watch him. "He's going to be a handsome one, don't you think, George? Not everyone appreciates the beauty of a raven. James, fetch me something from the kitchen. A bit of cooked egg or a piece of cheese."

"Cheese? Yes, sir."

"And don't you be touching nothing else in my kitchen," said Mrs. Hendricks.

James sprinted up the veranda stairs. Henry crouched lower and began speaking to the bird in a soothing tone. "That's a good fellow, now. You want to be friends, don't you? Let's just get you out of that box." The bird ruffled up its feathers. A hush as Henry put his hands around it, the raven meekly complying as he set it on the ground.

The raven lifted a foot, scratched the back of its head. Opened its mouth wide, like the inside of a pink-lined purse.

"See that, George? He wants to be fed. Hungry as anything. And trusting."

"I wouldn't have expected that," Mary said.

"Still," said Cook, "by my understanding, a raven is naught but a pest. Steals the songbirds' eggs."

"Prejudice and superstition," Henry said. "He's a living creature like any other, except that he's more clever than most."

James bounded down the stairs again. "Here's a piece of cheese and some lamb I cut up small."

"That's for the stew!" Cook said.

The bird made a plaintive rasping sound and opened its mouth again. Henry dropped the cheese and the beak snapped shut. A gulp. The mouth opened again. Next a bit of lamb. Snap and gulp.

"He wants more still," said the boy.

"Oh, he'll eat and eat. James, bring an empty cage from the shed. We'll take the bird up to my study. Mrs. Hendricks, if you would cook some egg and cut up some more meat."

"But I haven't got dinner half ready yet."

"I think this fellow is a good deal more needy than we are."

He turned as he heard Margaret's step behind him. She was coming down from the veranda, her hair loosely pinned. "What's all the excitement?" she said.

"Come and see the raven, dear."

As she approached the circle parted for her. The raven had closed its mouth and now turned its head to look at her. "Well, aren't you bold," she said. "Henry, I hope you're going to help this poor thing."

"Yes, of course. James is just going to get a cage." James immediately sprinted off. "I dare say it seems fascinated by you, Margaret. It hasn't taken its eyes away."

He saw her continue to look back at the bird. "Mary, we must have some of those nice gingersnaps Mrs. Hendricks baked yesterday. Do bring them out for the children, won't you, along with some lemonade."

The bird took an awkward yet dainty step towards her. It stretched out its head and softly squonked.

"Since he likes you so much," Henry said, "perhaps you should give him a name."

"I cannot."

"And why is that?"

"Because she already has a name."

"*She*? Why do you think the bird is a female? It's impossible to tell with young ravens. And what do you mean about it having a name, Margaret?"

She laughed uncomfortably. "I don't know. A woman's intuition, I suppose." He watched as she turned and went back to the house, lifting the hem of her skirt before the first stair.

He stood at the bar with a copy of the *Mail*. Before him appeared a coffee-coloured hand with a pink palm and crisp white sleeve, holding the glass of port. It had more presence, more *actuality* than his own hand.

"Thank you, Samuel."

"Yes, sir, Mr. Church. That's good aged port off the ship from Portugal that come up from New York. You want something else, just let me know."

The Negro moved away, polishing the bar with a cloth. A neat head and small ears. He was the only Negro in town and the club members considered themselves fortunate to employ him. He had come up from South Carolina, where his mother was a former house slave. Almost feminine in his movements. Yet every so often he would move his head a certain way and Henry would wonder if Africa still existed somewhere inside him. If so, what existed in himself? In anyone?

The room was warm. The evening was still quiet, just a foursome of men smoking and playing whist at one of the card tables, and old Woolwich, retired notary, fallen asleep in an armchair with an old issue of the *Dominion Illustrated Monthly* leaning on his damp chin. Henry did not especially like the club and was an indifferent drinker, but his father-in-law thought it was good for business to show himself as a regular sort. He was sure they all thought of him as the orphan risen above his station by Jeremiah Dawes. From inside his jacket he pulled out his pen, took off the cap, and checked the flow before sketching in the margin of the newspaper. He had an idea for a bicycle with a long and sharpened skate in front and two back wheels, which might be used to cross frozen lakes in winter. Even as he sketched, he idly read the article running alongside.

ANARCHIST THIEVES GIVE
OPPONENTS WHISKERS

Political Revolutionaries in Paris
Choose Ridicule over Bomb
From our European Correspondent

A gang of unusual political thieves, led by the notorious Armand Jacob, has embarrassed the municipal government of Paris by stealing dead rats and presenting them in the guise of city officials.

After the violent anarchist bombs and assassinations of recent years, including the knife attack on the Serbian minister and the bombing of the Café Terminus, the recent "Actions Théatrique" have come as a relief to Parisians and something of an entertainment as well. In this instance, rats, stuffed and preserved, were stolen from the display window of a ratcatcher in the Rue des Rosiers, whose sign stated that they had all been caught in the basement of the Paris City Hall. The anarchists took the rats and, breaking into City Hall under cover of night, placed them on the table around which the city's elected officials hold their meetings. Each was given the label of a politician's name and a distinguishing characteristic— a cigar held in a rat's claws, a miniature lorgnette, a walking stick. In the centre of the table a sign was placed stating "You Give Your Authority to Them."

While the mayor of Paris tried to hush up the mocking tableau, the Parisian newspapers had already been informed by anonymous letter, and several managed to publish sketches of the rats alongside portraits of their human counterparts. While it is uncertain just how this "action" will advance the cause of the anarchists, it does show that they are not without a sense of humour.

Meanwhile in Paris, the Universal Exhibition is finally beginning to draw larger numbers of visitors, if still not what had been initially predicted. Among the exposition highlights are the display of modern sculpture in the new Grand Palais, the recreation of medieval Paris, and the impressive demonstrations of German technical advancements. Most sensational in the field of arts has been the provocative dance performances of the American Louise Fuller. Unfortunately, heavy rain has caused damage to some pavilions.

He looked up; several men were coming noisily into the room, their voices raised and their spirits inflamed by drink. He recognized Ward and Gallagher from the coal company, a much younger man named Thomas Garnet, who had an assistant position at Arnott Soap, and bringing up the rear, George Beachcroft, who hailed Henry as they lined up along the bar.

"What a crushing blow," Gallagher was saying. A face like a potato left in the damp. "All hope is now extinguished."

"This is a bad sign, Garnet, very bad." George Beachcroft shook his head dismally. "Henry, tell our young friend that it's the beginning of the end for him. Give him the scientific point of view."

Samuel lined up glasses in front of them. "Good Canadian whisky. Right, Mr. Beachcroft?"

"Damn right."

Henry said, "I've no idea what you're speaking about, George."

"Garnet here has gotten himself engaged to one of the Hollenbeck daughters," said Ward.

"Not the fat one," said Gallagher loudly.

"Many congratulations." Henry reached out to shake Garnet's hand. The young man looked excessively grateful.

"Congratulations, my eye," George Beachcroft said. "We've been warning the poor dupe of the pull of the yoke, the tyranny of the institution. Just the other night, Garnet, we were speaking with envy of your position as a single man. And what do you do? Find yourself a bride. It's downright disheartening. I don't care what your evolutionists say, Henry, from what I can see men get not a whit smarter with time."

"But your own wives—"

George Beachcroft interrupted him. "Don't misunderstand us, Henry. You know that we admire our wives tremendously. Their social and cultural graces. Their devotion to home and children. We feel the deepest regard, and so on and so on."

"We would just prefer not to have them," said Gallagher, giggling.

"The expense!" said Ward. "I tell you, Garnet, if you are swallowing that old saw about two living as cheaply as one, then I'll sell you Niagara Falls for a dollar."

"But Theodora is so good at managing money."

"At managing to spend it, you mean. Those curtains must be changed, that china is not good enough for company, and please get your feet off the new ottoman. Suddenly you can do nothing right."

"It's very demoralizing," said George Beachcroft.

"And then there are the conversations," Gallagher went on. "You must discuss how Mrs. So-and-so does not know how to write a proper note of invitation, and cluck your tongue because the valet neglected to use oil of lavender on the bronzes. And just try talking seriously about politics. She'll want to, you know, but her sympathies are inane. These days it's always more rights for the female sex—"

"Except their own maids," said Ward.

"But you do not know my Theodora. She is not as you describe and never will be. To hear you speak this way is very insulting."

"Garnet," said George Beachcroft, "you've neglected to take off your hat."

"Whatever you do," Ward said, "do not let her read French novels."

"Absolutely right," said George Beachcroft. "Otherwise she'll turn out like that woman, Florence Maybrick. And you know how *her* husband ended up."

Gallagher whispered, "Arsenic."

"That really isn't funny."

"I shouldn't think so," George Beachcroft said thought-fully, then drank the remains of his whisky.

Henry felt himself gripping his own glass as if he would shatter it in his hand. A flush rose up from his neck. He would not prevent himself from speaking, he would not.

"I urge you not to listen to them, Mr. Garnet."

"Yes, I mean no, I will not."

"Women are not the baser half of humanity, but the finer. If the race as a whole listened to their feminine wisdom, the world would be a happier and more just place. If our wives find fault with us it is because we too often fall short of their rightful expectations. Worse, we underesti-mate both the complexities of their minds and the sub-tlety and depth of their emotions. It should not surprise us in the least that we disappoint them. If only we had higher expectations for ourselves. Just read Mill's *The Subjection of Women*—"

He saw them staring at him, Gallagher with his mouth half open. Henry turned his face to the bar. "In any case, that is my opinion."

Silence. George Beachcroft finally spoke. "Admirable passion, Henry. You are an example to us, even if we were just having some sport at Garnet's expense. And, of course, it is true that Mrs. Church is a model of beauty and intelligence."

"She is more than that."

"Samuel, pour us another. Why don't we make a toast to Mr. Garnet's forthcoming nuptials, about which we are all very glad."

"Hear, hear," said Ward.

As he rose up through sleep he slowly became aware of her absence from the bed. Reaching out, he felt only the cool sheets.

Immediately he was awake. He pulled off the covers and slipped his feet into the slippers by the bed. The house was its usual settling quiet. He opened the door and peered down the dark hall. Retreating back into the room, he went to the window.

The night sky above the willows had a scattering of stars. From the second floor he could not get a good view of the river, as it was obscured by the trees, but he could see the edge of the bank and also the wallpaper hanger's tent as an angular grey form. From somewhere below a man—the paper hanger—began singing.

I'll meet you under the moon tonight,
my darling Isabella.
I hope that we will spoon tonight,
my darling Isabella.

He tried to spot the paper hanger and found him weaving along the riverbank, his legs most clearly visible between the hanging willows. Now he stumbled, grasping a trunk and laughing, now he righted himself and began to sing again.

And if you will come away with me
the night will last for ever.
And if you promise to love only me—

A surprised cry, followed by a splash in the river. The paper hanger had fallen in. Henry could hear the man floundering about, flailing and sputtering. Quite possibly he couldn't swim. Henry was about to turn when something flashed between the trees. He heard more splashing, the sound of the paper hanger coughing river water out of his lungs as something sloshed towards the shore. He could see two shifting, indeterminate forms on the top of the bank behind the willows. The paper hanger sighed. The other form separated for a moment and then moved over him, and soon the sighs turned to low moans. Like one being, they moved rhythmically, as the paper hanger's moans grew more intense. Henry's face burned and his heart beat so hard he could no longer hear. He tried to force himself to turn away but he could not and stood by the window as the paper hanger cried out in ecstatic half-words that sounded both rapturous and bewildered.

Henry moved to the divan at the end of the bed, feeling his own body becoming paralyzed as if with some creeping venom. He did not know how long he sat in the dark, whether minutes or hours. The bedroom door opened and he saw Margaret, her hair wet against her face and her robe clinging damply.

"Henry."

She had whispered his name. He watched as she lowered herself slowly to one knee, wavered, then came down on the other. A beseeching look in her eyes before she collapsed onto the rug.

Doctor Walsh was dressed for dinner but nevertheless arrived on horseback, one of his well-known eccentricities.

While the doctor was in the bedroom examining Margaret, Henry paced the hallway, passing the mounted elk's head that had been shot by her father when a young man, the framed *cartes des visites* that had belonged to her late mother. Each minute was more unbearable than the last. He felt he must burst into the room. He tried to think of anything but Margaret, but all he could think of was Margaret, and all he could see was the dark moving form at the edge of the river. He had to stop himself from pounding his fist against his forehead.

He tried to think of anything he knew of her, anything besides tonight. Once she had told him that at the age of ten she swooned while listening to Dwight L. Moody during a tent revival. Her father carried her senseless body up to the podium, where the preacher revived her with a bottle of smelling salts that he kept in his breast pocket. But it was useless; he could not help thinking of what he had seen by the river. But what had he really seen? It was not clear, he might have been mistaken. He ought not to believe what common sense told him could not be true.

The doctor emerged from the room, closing the door softly behind him. Henry rushed at him. "Please, tell me how she is."

"Let us step away from the door. I don't believe it is a serious episode. Heart palpitations, a mildly elevated temperature, an inability to keep down food. I do not believe it is anything more than a temporary nervous condition brought on by some sudden excitement. A little laudanum will help her sleep. And give her a dose of camphor-julep and water in the day. Did the two of you have an argument?"

He hesitated. "No, there was nothing. Doctor Walsh, I am more anxious than I can say. Will she be all right?"

The doctor smiled reassuringly and placed his hand on Henry's arm. "You must not blame yourself, Henry. These little episodes are perhaps a sign that she has not yet found her way to full and calm maturity. Do not be overly concerned by their increase. I have known Margaret since just after her mother died. She has always been a sweet-tempered and yet enigmatic girl. To be frank, any husband would have found her less than ideally malleable to the demands of the married state. If I might ask, is it possible that you are too indulgent to her whims? Too sympathetic?"

"I do not think so."

"As you say. Well, let her rest the night. Be sure that she is kept company by her maid or yourself. Don't worry, Henry. I'm sure the episodes will grow less frequent again with time. One last piece of advice. Don't wear that mournful expression in her presence. It certainly won't help matters."

The doctor pulled on his gloves as Henry accompanied him to the front door, where the groom had his horse ready. The doctor mounted his chestnut bay with energy and slapped its hindquarters so that it galloped down the dark path, throwing up gravel.

The first man to ascend in a balloon was a young French naturalist named François Pilâtre de Rozier, who rose in a fire-balloon anchored by ropes to the ground on October 15, 1783. Two years later he died while trying to cross the English Channel. This last fact Henry chose not to tell Margaret.

The balloonist who had set up his air vehicle on the lawn came from Philadelphia and had the name of Staunch. Travelled the fair circuit. Wore a modified horseback-riding outfit, with round goggles over his eyes, and chewed tobacco. Henry had to climb into the pannier with the help of a short ladder, and as he stepped over the side the pannier bobbed sideways, causing him to momentarily lose his balance. He would have preferred not to make a public exhibition of himself, but a hot-air balloon the size of an elephant could not go unnoticed. Besides the household staff and, of course, Margaret, who was holding her hands together very still, there were George and Althea Beachcroft, their children, several other acquaintances from town and a dozen or so workers from the Dawes factory who had asked permission to watch. Among them stood Giancarlo Caporale, in a dusty black suit, running a finger thoughtfully over his goat's tuft.

George Beachcroft called: "Don't expect me to catch you if you fall." Althea banged his shin with her parasol.

"Do I need goggles as well?" Henry asked the balloonist. He found himself unnaturally raising his voice.

"Nah," Staunch said. "They're just for show. You ready?"

At that moment the raven hopped onto the rim of the pannier. It looked at Henry, waggled its head, and made a series of clicks. As a subject for the study of natural behaviour, it had proven hopeless. Spent the mornings in the kitchen perched atop the flour urn, flapping down to steal currants that cook used in her baking. In the evenings it waited on the roof of the turret for Henry to come down the road on his bicycle.

"We don't need your help in the air," Henry said to the bird. "Go on, now."

The bird clucked, shook itself, and made a gargling sound before swooping back to the veranda. Staunch added fuel to the brazier, making the flames rise. "Do be careful," Margaret called. She came forwards and reached up so that Henry might take her slim hand for a moment. The concern that showed in her eyes made her only more exquisite. She seemed so clearly herself again, had recovered so quickly from her nervous condition, that he was almost free of his own fears. And how could he be afraid of a little trip around the countryside? The famous Vaulx had just floated across Europe. It had been one of his boyhood dreams, soaring aloft over the earth.

"Throw off the lines!" Staunch shouted dramatically.

Four of the workmen came forwards, Giancarlo among them. Henry leaned towards him and said, "What do you think, Giancarlo? Would your fellow anarchists approve?"

The Italian smiled. "Of course, Boss. We believe in progress. Never perfection, but always progress. And besides, a man who can rise into air is above all authority."

"I have been meaning to ask you something. I read in the newspaper about an incident in Paris involving the mayor and some rats."

Giancarlo grinned. "Ah, Armand. He is a rare one."

"You actually know him?"

He made a pretence of suppressing a grin. "I do not know anybody. I am just an employee of the Dawes family. May you enjoy your ride, Boss."

"All right, let's go," Staunch said impatiently. He counted to three and the workmen unhitched the tethers. The balloon rose more suddenly than Henry had expected, the pannier lurching to one side before levelling again. In moments the human figures below grew small; he could see Margaret shading her eyes as she looked up. He waved to her in a deliberately jolly manner.

The river was more winding than he had realized, despite his having seen it on a map. On the road to town an automobile pulled over and the passengers got out to watch. And there was the town itself, the toy buildings set among the green and around them the cultivated fields like a quilt. Perhaps this was what he wanted, to be lifted out of the realm of human struggle, desire, woe. He raised his gaze to the air about them, so white, so blue. The absence of sound broken by the unmistakable honking of Canada geese, flying in ragged formation just yards away, their wing beats steady as a metronome.

"Rather pleasant up here, don't you think?" Staunch called.

But Henry didn't wish to speak. He reached his hand into a cloud.

They remained in the air for under an hour. Because of the lack of wind they drifted only a quarter mile, coming down in a field of immature corn. One of the factory workers drove Staunch's wagon to the side road, and Henry helped to deflate the balloon and load its dismantled parts into the back. Refreshments waited for them on the lawn, although the remaining factory workers had already returned to work. They all asked him at once what the experience had been like, and he told them it was exhilarating, but the truth was, there had, in the end, been something disappointing about it. Perhaps it was simply that he had been a mere passenger. Margaret was the only one who did not ask him anything. Passing him on the lawn she brushed his fingers with her own.

SUMMER 1900

*I*s not the inventor greater than the poet, the soldier, and even the statesman? The poet writes of a better world, the soldier fights for it, the statesman argues over it. But it is the inventor who provides greater ease and comfort, pleasure and happiness. It is the inventor who increases wealth, who permits the poet to disseminate his work, who arms the soldier, who provides the means for the statesman to alter the nation by means of railways and bridges and electrification...

He put down the printed copy of the speech made at the last Toronto meeting, which Chester had sent to him. Scrawled in the margin was Chester's own comment: *Are we not then merely servants of those in power?* And what did Henry himself believe? Certainly nothing so grand. He had developed no theories of the inventive mind nor ever waxed eloquent over the visionary nature of invention, even to Margaret. His thoughts had always been practical: how power might be transferred from pedal to wheel with less loss, how a gear system might be simplified. That was the nature of his poetic soul.

He had arrived home early, hoping to surprise Margaret, but her maid had informed him that her mistress had gone for a walk to gather wildflowers for the table. So he had come up to the turret, not to think about inventions but to consider preparing another puppet show for the town children, a small entertainment to add to the Dominion Day celebrations. He was thinking of something by Andersen; a volume of his tales had been one of his few possessions in the orphanage. "The Steadfast Tin Soldier" perhaps, unless it was too solemn. It was a curiosity to himself that, for all his modesty, he treated these little performances quite seriously. They were offerings he felt some quiet yet undeniable urge to give, for his own sake as much as for the children. Perhaps they were something like the dreams he had had as a boy, lying awake in bed, hearing the sound of other boys breathing. Dreams of performing some heroic act or of learning that his parents were of noble blood and had come to rescue him. Or of simply escaping, opening the window and lifting into the air on wings made of paper and wax and feathers taken from pillows.

The raven flew in through the centre window, skidding upon the desk. It held a sparkling bit of quartz in its mouth, which it deposited upon his sketching paper, afterwards plumping up its feathers. Henry picked up the quartz and put it in the open cigar box where he kept the bird's "treasures": a bent coin, a mussel shell, a broken bracelet, coloured stones, buttons, an empty bromide packet.

The bird began to preen, stretching out a wing. Henry took up his pen and sketched it in outline, then a series of mechanical rods inside, as if it were an artificial contrivance rather than a living thing. Most inventors had given up using birds as a model for flight experiments. Instead, they were trying propellers and fixed wings in double or triple sets with engines powered by steam or coal or, most recently, gasoline. But he was not yet ready to give up the beauty of the idea. He opened a drawer, took out a sweet, and tossed it to the raven, who snatched it in its beak. Then he pushed back his chair and rose.

He came down the stairs to see if Margaret had returned. On reaching the second floor he heard a continuous but muffled sound and it took him a moment, standing on the Scottish carpet that ran the length of the hall, to realize that it was the bath water running. It was uncharacteristic of Margaret to be taking a bath in the middle of the afternoon; likely she had got muddy gathering her flowers. He looked down the hall to see if there were any servants about before creeping towards the bathroom door. He could hear her singing. She had a lovely voice, a little thin and not perfectly pitched but somehow entrancing, and he leaned against the door to hear better. Just listening, knowing she was washing herself in the filling bath, aroused him. How much he wanted to see the picture of her there, arm or foot raised, soaping herself. He could not resist turning the knob and inching the door open. Her voice became clearer, as did the sound of the running water. She had not put on the electric light but had lit a candle instead, and the flickering illumination revealed the contours of the tiled wall with its climbing vine pattern along the side of the tub. And then rising from the tub he saw something fan-shaped and darkly iridescent, something glistening with water—

A scream.

He quickly shut the door. "I—I am sorry, dear Margaret, I should not have—"

The door opened, requiring him to step back. Margaret stood there, her robe so wet that he could see the shape of her nipples through the silk. She tried to smile at him, but her face was pale and trembling and she was breathing hard.

"You are not ill, Margaret?"

"No, I'm fine. You startled me, Henry. I'm glad to see you. If you give me a moment, I will get dressed."

He stood aside to let her by. She walked unsteadily on her bare feet, leaving damp footprints up to the door of their bedroom, which she closed softly behind her.

"Let me sing it for you, Mr. Church. We had a Jewish fellow up in New York write it for us, a real Tin Pan Alley type."

Henry listened as Krebbs played on the office piano, an upright left over from his father-in-law's five years in the piano business, before he sold out to Nordheimer. The tune was called "The Dawes Two-Wheeler Waltz," and it sounded like a hundred other songs he had heard. Perhaps not even as good. Still, they would publish the sheet music and give it away at their pavilion at the Toronto Industrial Exhibition in the fall. His father-in-law was right; they had to do something. For three or four years they had hardly been able to keep up with demand, but now sales continued to drop each month from the previous year. And now their major competitors—Massey-Harris, Gendron, Lozier—had responded by merging to form CCM, and their bicycles were crowding out Dawes in the stores that the company didn't own itself. Maybe Dawes had too many models, or their quality made their prices still too high; everyone else was slashing theirs. Or they ought to begin manufacturing sleds and baby carriages.

Or if he could just come up with one practical innovation.

The raven stood on the piano, causing Krebbs to glance up nervously as he played. When the song was over, the bird shook itself violently and let out a doglike yip. Henry dismissed Krebbs and went back to the sheaf of reports from the western salesmen. In the margins he had sketched a new idea, a sturdy tricycle with solid rubber wheels and moulded letters in reverse, like printing type. A tank of ink sat behind the rider's seat with a feed tube to a set of rollers that would run against the wheels, so that as the tricycle moved the inked-up tires would print two parallel lines of advertising upon the road. *Follow these words to the Dawes Bicycle Store.* And they could sell the vehicle to others. *Wear our support shoes and your feet will float over this road.* In all likelihood his father-in-law would dismiss the idea, as he had rejected Henry's last dozen with only a cursory glance. *What we need is an improved bicycle, not some novelty device fit for the circus...*

A shout made him turn to the window that looked down upon the factory floor. With so many workers in so many warrenlike departments it took him a long minute to find the two figures standing at the far end of the centre aisle. The aisle was used for the wagons of frames, hubs, gears, and sundry other parts that needed to be moved along, but the wagon coming down now, pushed by a worker, had halted. Of the two figures confronting each other, one was Giancarlo Caporale, as he could tell by the maroon cap. The other appeared younger and taller, but Henry could not identify him. Where was the foreman, MacMurtrie?

The younger man pushed Giancarlo's shoulder, causing him to take a step back. Other workers started to gather. Henry disliked these altercations between employees, the motives for which were impossible to comprehend. But Giancarlo had never been involved in one before and had often resolved disputes before they turned dangerous. He was looked up to by the others, no matter what their politics.

Yes, now he saw who the young man was; the new fellow, who came from a town in Italy near Giancarlo's. He seemed to recall that the young man had been staying with Giancarlo and his family. The same young man who now snatched something—a screwdriver or wrench—from a table and jabbed it towards Giancarlo.

The raven squawked and fluttered up as Henry sprang to the door. He moved so quickly down the winding iron staircase leading to the factory floor that he missed a rung and banged his knee on the rail. He sprinted down the aisle, pushed past the wagon, wheel rims spilling, and looked up again just as Giancarlo swung a set of handlebars, cracking the young man on the side of his head. The man fell to his knees, his hands going up to his ear. Giancarlo brought the handlebar down on his skull. Then he kicked the curled body in the side.

He was done by the time Henry reached them. Giancarlo took out a leather pouch and calmly rolled tobacco into a cigarette paper. The young man lay still, a trickle of blood running from his ear. Two workmen tried to pick him up, but the young man screamed and they let go.

MacMurtrie arrived panting. He was a lanky Scot with enormous mutton chops. "Damnation. You're a primitive lot of savages. I'm very sorry, Mr. Church, but I was in the other building getting the kinks out of that new chain-wheel stamping machine. Look at the poor wretch. He won't be much use to us now."

"Please send for a doctor, Mr. MacMurtrie. Have the men move him carefully to the lunch benches. And you, Giancarlo. Up to my office."

"Yes, Boss."

"And put that cigarette away."

"Bloody Italians," MacMurtrie muttered. "More hot-headed than the Irish."

Henry did not turn around, although he could hear Giancarlo's footsteps on the iron steps behind him, until he was behind his own desk. He deliberately sat down, letting the older man stand before him. Still on the piano, the raven opened one eye at them and closed it again.

"You might have killed that young man."

"I think of maybe killing him. But I decide, no."

"But why? What could have motivated you?"

"This is a thing that is private."

"I see. This is the result of your political ideologies. Your superior beliefs about the oppressive nature of authority and the rights of each of us to make our own moral choices. Calling yourself an anarchist gives you the right to beat a man half to death."

Giancarlo rubbed the white stubble on his chin. "No, it does not." He sighed. "What I do now, it is a failing. I understand this the whole time. It is not always easy to take out the old beliefs and bring inside the new. It is a long struggle to make ourselves free. I too am not free."

"Then you at least regret what you have done."

"As an anarchist, yes, I regret it. As a man . . ."

He did not finish the sentence but shrugged instead. "All right," he said, and he removed his cap and ran his fingers through the goat's tuft of hair. "I tell you because I do not wish you to reject anarchism for what I have done. This other man, I help to bring him over. I let him sleep in my house, I find him this job. And in my house this man gives a letter to my wife. My wife is younger than me, my first wife die on the boat coming to Canada. He gives her this letter and she throws it in the trash. I find this letter. She does not want it. If she wants it, then I certainly kill him."

He did not look away from Henry as he spoke. But now Henry looked down at his desk. "I see. The same age-old jealousy."

"Not just that, Boss. Because this I understand and forgive. But it is the treating of my wife as something that I own, as a possession—this is what I condemn in myself. It goes so deeply against what I believe. If I am to be free, then I must treat others as equally free. But I do not."

Henry stood up but he did not look again at Giancarlo. Instead he went to the window and stared down at the factory floor, where MacMurtrie had sent the men back to work. "Fighting is forbidden on the factory premises. The penalty is firing. That is Mr. Dawes' rule. Besides, if I don't fire you, the other workers will see me as weak. They see me that way already."

"But this they will not see as a weakness. They will nod their heads and understand what a man must do. And that you accept it."

Now he looked at Giancarlo. "But don't you think you deserve punishment?"

"Punishment, no. That is only the exercise of authority. I must find my own atonement."

"And how will you do that?"

"First, by letting him stay until he is better. Then I must help him to make his own life somewhere else."

"To work for one of my competitors."

Again he shrugged.

"All right. You will lose two days' pay. Let the men know that too. You're finished for today."

"Yes, Boss."

He nodded his head. Then, as if remembering something, he put his hand into his jacket pocket and pulled out a book. "I brought you something else to read. Kropotkin. But it is in English. You know him? Born a real prince but he said, 'No more, I will be just like everyone else.'"

"This is not the day for it, Giancarlo."

"I leave it anyway. These men who write, they are a better example than I am."

He put it on the sill of the window and went out.

The mayor made a speech on the podium opposite the town hall—*When our great land became a nation unto itself thirty-three years ago*—but Henry could not listen to the words. The bleachers that had been raised to watch the fireworks on the other side of the river were crowded and rambunctious, and when he turned he could see in the near darkness the glint of flasks being passed between the young men in the upper rows. Down near the bottom the children in their best clothes held little flags or engravings of Laurier given out by the local Liberal newspaper. He did not much enjoy such scenes, but he could be patient and did not have the same aversion to crowds that made Margaret fidget so on their bench.

George Beachcroft was leaning over and whispering something about the mayor, and Althea was smiling, but he had missed what George said. His mind had been reviewing the puppet show he had given in the garden for their friends' children, not "The Steadfast Tin Soldier" but instead "The Ugly Duckling." The swan puppet had been received with pleasing gasps, which had been repeated when the creature spread its wings, but there had been a stretch in the middle that had dragged on a little too long.

While the mayor was still speaking a loud crack sounded across the river and a streak of silvery sparks arced upwards, making the crowd cheer. Someone had cued the fireworks too soon. The mayor tried to continue, but more fireworks followed, a deafening series of bangs and showers of red and blue sparks over the water, and he threw up his hands and came down from the podium.

An acrid smoke descended upon them. Several of the younger children were crying in fear and hiding in their mothers' laps. Margaret stood up suddenly and Henry followed suit, momentarily losing his balance and almost falling backwards over the bench.

"It is too loud for me," she said. "I'll meet you on Main Street."

"Of course I will come with you."

But she put her hand on his shoulder a moment to show that he should stay. He sat down again but could not remain, and although George Beachcroft was in the middle of telling some story about the mayor's brother, he got up and made his way down from the bleachers. Margaret had got ahead of him and he could not see her as he passed a group of young men smoking behind the stands. He went up to Prince Street, past Jameson's Millinery, the fire hall, Stillwell Dry Goods, Finch's Lane. As he reached Main Street he saw her, standing on the boardwalk and looking at a large theatrical bill pasted up by the Victoria Theatre.

When he came up beside her, she did not turn around but a shift in the way she stood acknowledged his presence.

First Appearance
of the World's MOST powerful STRONGMAN
COUNT ANATOLE BELINSKY
Member of the Russian Aristocracy
Acclaimed by the Royal Families of Russia, England, and Sweden
for his Phenomenal feats of STRENGTH and ENDURANCE.
Also known as
THE HUMAN WHALE
for his Wondrous Display of LUNG POWER
and NATURAL GRACE
in the world's LARGEST AQUATHEATRE
in a Performance of both SCIENTIFIC and ARTISTIC value.
Also, the most amusing SHADOWGRAPHY demonstration
as studied under the great TREWEY of Paris.
VICTORIA THEATRE
One Week Only, July 3–10
Tickets $2.00, $1.00, and 50 cents
Programs, Photographic Postcards,
Souvenirs available in the theatre lobby

He said, "We don't usually get that sort of nonsense here. It sounds more appropriate for the Egyptian Hall in London. I don't suppose he'll attract much of a crowd."

She did not answer for a moment, seemed not really to see him. She said, "I think we might go. Just to see something different. We could ask the Beachcrofts to come with us."

"Do you think they would want to? You know they refuse to go anywhere that isn't socially exclusive."

"But then they could hardly go anywhere in this town! No, let's not walk on, Henry. Let's wait until they come. You'll see. I understand Althea better than you do."

"You understand everybody better than I do."

She gave him her loveliest smile.

The fireworks must have been over, for people were moving up the street now, couples arm in arm and young men running and shouting to one another. Carriages began to raise dust as they rattled by. He did not find anything to say and so they waited until the Beachcrofts finally appeared, George swinging his walking stick.

"Don't blame me," he said on coming up. "I've never seen anyone take so long to adjust a hat in my life. For the life of me, Althea, I can see no difference from before."

"You see what I must live with?" Althea said. "A man with not the slightest appreciation for female dress."

"Yes, but you adore me anyway, don't you, buttercup?"

He attempted to take her round the waist. "Oh, go on! We're not courting, for heaven's sake. What's this? A new show at the theatre?"

"Yes, we were just reading it," Margaret said.

"A strongman? How delicious. And dunked in water, no less. We absolutely must go, Margaret. And let's not bring our husbands unless they promise to behave."

Margaret smiled at her husband again, and he showed in his own expression that he was perfectly content to be proven wrong.

He was surprised at the crush to get into the theatre, the front doors jammed with people from every level of society.

He recognized some faces from the factory, the men in their Sunday clothes with their wives on their arms, unsure whether they might take off their hats to him. Likely they had not seen a more ornate interior—velvet and brass and fancy plasterwork of cherubs and lyres—even in their churches. They might have been in New York or London instead of their own town.

Margaret clung tightly to his arm; the press of the crowd unnerved her. In the lobby, hawkers were waving programs and postcard photographs. George Beachcroft said, "It's too infernally hot in here. I'm going to get us all something to drink. Henry, you take the ladies to the box."

George slipped into the crowd. Someone jostled Margaret, making her gasp. "Are you all right?" Henry said. "Perhaps you would rather go home."

"No, it's all right. I am just silly sometimes."

They came hard upon Oscar Leland, the Englishman who had built the Victoria and now filled it with touring theatricals, concerts, and singers. Henry had to stop himself from raising an eyebrow at the purple-and-green-striped waistcoat that Leland wore over his substantial girth. "How splendid of you to come, Mr. and Mrs. Church, Mrs. Beachcroft. You raise the tone of our opening. This Russian fellow is proving to be quite a draw. He may not be Sir Henry Irving, but he leaves the audience immensely satisfied. I've brought him up from Boston at considerable expense. End of his American tour. Quite spectacularly successful. Perhaps you would care to be introduced to Count Belinsky after the performance? A rough sort of fellow for royalty, but charming in his way. Ah, there's the bell. Which seats have you got? Very good, you'll see everything."

Henry ushered the women up the staircase to their box, pulling aside the curtain. In the orchestra and gallery people were still shifting, getting settled. George arrived with their drinks, ginger beer for the women and lager for the men. "That Leland's a cheapskate. He ought to have more waiters for the boxes."

"Did you hear?" Althea said. "We are to go backstage. That's the term, isn't it? How daring."

"To fawn on a performer," George said. "Aren't you just tingling with excitement, Henry?"

In truth he was tired, having risen early to see to the aviary. Usually his eyes closed before any show was half over. Perhaps Margaret wouldn't like it and they could slip away at the intermission.

From the pit an organ began to play. The electric lights dimmed without being extinguished. The melody rose to a crescendo and the curtains parted to reveal the strongman, bathed in blue light. Feet firmly planted, hands powerfully crossed against his chest, he glared at the audience as if he were furious with them. He was rather short but everything about him evoked an aura of strength. His legs, clad in the leotard of an acrobat, had thighs like tree trunks. His arms were enormous. Even his head, absolutely bald but with heavy eyebrows, looked powerful.

No one applauded; evidently he made the audience feel too apprehensive.

The strongman lifted one hand and then pointed to the side. Instantly a light illuminated a blacksmith's anvil on the stage.

"I need...a man!"

He had a heavy accent, which somehow added to the

primitiveness of him. "I need a man who believes he is strong. Come on, come on! Don't you want to show off for the ladies?"

A scattering of laughter, but the strongman himself did not smile. A man in the front row stood up. "Excellent. There is always one out there. Come up the stairs at the side of the stage. That's right. There is nothing to be afraid of. At least, nothing that I will admit to. Well—" he looked out at the audience with impatience. "Does this volunteer not deserve a round of applause?"

The clapping was excessive, as if people were afraid of further disapproval. The man who came up was wearing a double-breasted tweed suit that looked too small for him. He was a good four or five inches taller than the strong-man, and rather broad himself. "Very good," said the strongman. "Now tell us, sir, what is your name?"

His answer was too low for Henry to hear.

"Please speak up, sir."

"Archibald Legg."

"And what is your profession, Mr. Legg?"

"I head a crew doing rail line repairs for the Canadian Pacific."

"That sounds like a job requiring considerable strength."

"Some would say so."

"Excellent. Then you are just the man. Do me a small favour and lift up that anvil, will you? I've accidentally left a ten-dollar bill under it."

A few titters. The strongman proceeded to examine his nails, as if bored, but the man named Legg merely stared at the anvil. The audience laughed, more genuinely this time. Margaret laughed too.

"Are you holding it up yet?" the count asked, looking now at the nails on his other hand. The man did not answer but walked slowly to the anvil. He crouched down, put his arms around it, and heaved.

It did not budge.

The man tried again, straining harder. His face darkened, a low moan came from him, but the anvil did not move.

He let go, caught his breath. "It's too heavy for any man."

Only now did the count look up in surprise. "Is it? I didn't realize. Perhaps you require some help. Would anyone like to assist Mr. Legg?"

A second man came up. The first fellow, Legg, was clearly uneasy about trying again, but seemed to feel he had no choice, as if the strongman had authority over him. They got on either side and heaved together without the slightest effect. A third man was called up, then a fourth and fifth. It was impossible for them all to grasp the anvil at once, so the new recruits had to hold onto the old. It was quite ridiculous and one of them actually fell onto his backside.

The audience was truly laughing now. On Henry's other side, George made snorting noises.

"All right," said the strongman. "I do not want you to hurt yourselves. Please move aside." The five men huddled desultorily on the right side of the stage while the strongman crouched down and wrapped his arms around the anvil. He grunted with effort.

Nothing.

He shouted and strained.

Nothing.

He screamed, his face contorting horribly. The anvil rose an inch, perhaps two. Another yell and he straightened his legs. A third and he hefted the anvil over his head.

Great cheers.

He dropped the anvil down again, several feet from its original resting place. Then he picked up the ten-dollar bill that had indeed been beneath it and held it out to the audience. "I would give this to you, Mr. Legg," he said, tucking it into his leotard. "But I am afraid it will prove too heavy for you."

Next, two assistants wheeled a long, shallow trough of water onto the stage. They brought out a heavy rope, looping one end around the strongman's waist. Then male volunteers were invited onto the stage; Henry recognized two of them from his factory. "Do you think ten against one is fair?" the strongman asked the audience. "No? Perhaps you're right. Let's bring up two more." A tug-of-war ensued, the twelve men on one side and the count on the other, each moving forwards towards the water and then at the last moment hauling back again. At one point the count was so close that his knuckles touched the water. But with a sudden and seemingly inhuman gathering of strength, he pulled back inch by inch, never losing ground again, his opponents sliding helplessly forwards, pushing into one another, until the first two toppled into the trough.

Henry looked at Margaret. She did not applaud or even move, but kept her hands clasped tightly. He could not read her face, beyond an obvious keen interest. "Margaret?" She looked at him and smiled, and he smiled with her.

More feats of strength followed. Barbells of increasing weights. Smashing through lengths of wood. Bending iron into a knot. There was little sense to the order of the performance, and none of these feats seemed as impressive as the first two, but still this Balinsky held the attention of the audience. Some novelty effects came next: the flinging of autographed cards from the stage to the most distant seats, followed by some merely competent juggling. Here the audience began to cough and shift about. The organ music swelled and a white backdrop was unfurled while an assistant brought out a projecting lantern. In the circle of light cast on the backdrop, the strongman performed his shadowgraphy, positioning his hands and sometimes using tiny props—a stick with a string attached, various shapes of pasteboard—to create a series of images: a fisherman in his boat, a janitress knocking a broom onto the head of one of her tenants, a ballet dancer turning. The last was a man dropping from the gallows.

The curtain fell on the first act.

"It's deathly hot in here," Althea Beachcroft said. "I can't be the only one who wants an ice. Margaret?"

"Yes, it is hot."

"It's your turn, Henry," said George. "I'll be damned if you can find the boy who is supposed to be serving us."

"I'll just go down," Henry said. He left the box and worked through the crowd on the stairway. He could not understand how a man, even one who appeared as strong as this Russian, could lift an anvil that must have weighed hundreds of pounds. At the stand in the lobby there was a considerable wait, followed by the struggle back up. By the time he entered the box, the ices were half melted in their cups. Margaret, her hand on Althea's arm, was laughing at something her friend had said.

"This big fellow has an odd assortment of tricks." George spooned up the ice. "Actually, he strikes me as more the Germanic type than Russian."

"In my opinion," said Althea, "it is worth the entrance fee to see that gentleman in a leotard."

"Do you hear what my wife just said? Althea, I would be only too happy to model a leotard for you any evening. I am no weakling myself, you know. Come, feel this muscle in my arm."

"I politely decline. Did I see you volunteering to pull that rope? You've dripped ice on your beard. Give me your handkerchief."

"I can do it myself. And as for the rope, I didn't want to embarrass the chap. After all, he must make his living."

Henry had listened to their friends with a smile intended to express amusement, but he was waiting for Margaret's opinion. She had been eating her own ice a very little at a time and watching the stage as the curtain billowed out here and there from the movement behind it. Now she said, "This interlude is awfully long."

"No doubt the count is taking a nap to restore his strength. Eh, Henry?"

"Are you enjoying it, Margaret?" Henry asked.

"Well, it is very silly, isn't it? And I'm sorry, Althea, but that leotard makes the man look ridiculous. And he has so little natural poise on the stage. I almost feel sympathy for him."

"At last," George said as the lights began to dim.

They settled back in their chairs as the organ played a lugubrious, almost funereal melody. As the first and then a second curtain rose there was a scattering of applause; on the stage stood a six-sided glass tank, the edges reinforced with steel, much like a giant version of the home aquaria that had become fashionable for a time. Henry estimated its length at fifteen feet or more and its height at twenty. It must have held ten thousand gallons of water, the surface of which rose to just a few inches from the top, and it was otherwise empty but for a large clamshell, no doubt artificial, in the distant lower corner, which slowly opened to release a few bubbles of air before closing again.

The music continued as coloured lights began to play through the water from above. Without warning there was a splash; it took Henry a moment to realize that the strongman had dived into the tank, sending up a spray. He hit the bottom with both hands flat and his body seemed to go limp. Slowly the strongman stirred, shaking his head back and forth, letting out a stream of bubbles from his mouth. His bathing costume clung to his muscular frame.

He did not come up for air but began to swim near the bottom, from one end to the other. He paused at each corner, and when he came to the clamshell he waited for it to open and then put his head into it for a moment. Then he continued to swim, moving with far greater elegance than he had on land, and although it seemed unlikely that he could hear the organ, his movements coincided with the music in a surprisingly artistic fashion.

"An underwater ballet," George said. "Unfortunately, I hate the ballet."

"Shh," said Althea and Margaret together.

The strongman rose slowly to the surface. His head above the water, he called out, "A slate!" Two assistants hurried onto the stage, one carrying a ladder and the other the slate and chalk that had been called for. With the ladder placed against the side of the tank, the assistant flung himself up its rungs and handed the items to the strongman. The assistants removed the ladder from the stage.

Bobbing at the surface, the strongman spoke in short bursts. "A series of predictions and secrets." He seemed already breathless. "The shell whispers them to me. I cannot tell you who these predictions are meant for. Only you yourselves can know."

Down into the water he plunged. He swam immediately to the shell, putting his head inside it for a moment. Then, hovering near the bottom, he wrote upon the slate. It had to be some kind of special chalk. He moved towards the front glass and pressed the slate against it.

You have not told
your loved ones
who you really are

A rise of murmurs from the audience. Back to the clamshell he went. Erasing the first with his hand, he wrote another.

The fortune
you have been seeking
is already on its way
to you

George whispered, "Well, that could be for any of us, what? It is too easy."

"You want to spoil everything," said Althea. "Now hush."

More predictions came rapidly, the strongman flashing each for only a moment before turning back to the shell.

The man you secretly
fear is plotting against you

The great risk you are
considering will save one
and ruin another

Kindness will come
from an unexpected
quarter

Not once did he come to the surface to breathe, an impossibly long time. The audience too seemed to hold its breath; here and there among the shadowed faces Henry could hear a sudden gasping for air. The strongman swam again to the shell, listened by placing his ear inside it, then withdrew and violently shook his head. He listened once more, shook his head again, swam to the opposite corner of the tank. But after a minute or so he returned, listened a final time, and though he shook his head mournfully, he wrote on the slate.

Your life
will never be the same
after today

Even as Henry read the words, a movement at the clamshell caught his eye. Something dark was emerging from inside it. People in the audience began to whisper and point. Nervous laughter broke out and then quickly died again. The emerging thing rose up, almost balloonlike but for an unfolding appendage, and another, and as it turned it showed a white fathomless eye.

"My Lord," said Althea.

An octopus, although of course it could not be a real one. Still, it certainly was a clever artificial creation made of supple India rubber and with some advanced gear mechanism inside. It looked astonishingly lifelike as it rose beyond the shell, unfurling its tentacled arms and raising them menacingly upwards. The strongman acted unaware of its presence; he was still holding the slate up to the glass. Even Henry had a desire to cry out a warning, and it came to him that the last prediction—*Your life will never be the same after today*—was intended for the strongman himself. Several people actually began to shout, and a man in the first row jumped from his seat and began to climb onto the stage before an assistant rushed out from the wing to send him back.

Margaret screamed.

So did many other women, including Althea. For the octopus had attacked the strongman, thrusting several arms around his head and shoulders and dragging him back. The strongman dropped the slate and chalk and struck out ineffectually at the entwining arms. Turning, he became only more entangled, his legs too being caught up. The two entwined forms began to move about the tank as they did battle, but the strongman never seemed to gain the upper hand. Surely he needed to breathe, but he could not get near the surface or even the shell. The audience rose to its feet, shouting, calling for the assistants to intervene.

The decorum of the theatre had turned to chaos. The strongman thrashed back and forth, throwing the creature's body against the glass and causing waves to break over the tank's surface and crash over the sides.

A voice rose above the din: "A weapon! The count needs a weapon!"

The two assistants came onto the stage, one carrying the ladder, another holding up a knife with a blade that reflected the stage light. Even before the ladder was set against the tank the assistant was scrambling onto it, and when he was just over halfway up he tossed the knife high into the air. The blade glinted brightly as it turned over and over, arcing over the side and falling into the tank.

It sunk down through the water behind the strongman. He had not seen it drop! Pandemonium in the audience. Shrieks of terror. The creature and the strongman tumbled head over heels and the glint caught the strongman's eye. He tried to pull towards the knife, but the octopus only held him tighter in its grip. A new struggle began, man and creature embracing one another, rolling through the water. The strongman managed to free a hand, then his arm, and he reached along the bottom of the tank, missing the knife by mere inches. He tried again, and again missed. He tried once more, touched the handle, but only succeeded in pushing it an inch or two farther away. Terrible groans from the audience. A final reach, pulling the octopus along with all his strength, and his fingers were on the knife. He had it! But at the same moment a slender arm of the octopus wrapped around his wrist. The knife plunged between them, but who was in control of it as they struggled Henry could not tell. They turned slowly in the centre of the tank and a dark cloud bloomed between them.

Blood.

The water turned red. The strongman seemed to weaken as the two struggling forms became less and less visible. And then they could not be seen at all. The audience had become silent except for quiet sobbing here and there.

They waited.

"Get a doctor!" A woman's grief-stricken voice.

An explosion of water at the surface. And then, slipping down the front of the tank, water cascading onto the stage, was the strongman. He fell to the ground and with difficulty picked himself up and raised his arms triumphantly.

Wild applause, hooting, cheers. "My word," George shouted over the noise. "I've never seen anything like that."

Henry looked at Margaret. She, too, was standing, the slightest smile on her face.

"Althea, love, please say something. Come on, old girl." George leaned over his wife, tapping his hands repeatedly on her pale cheeks. Henry saw that she had fainted.

They were all turned to her now. Althea opened her eyes, blinked in confusion, and pushed her husband away. "Don't stare at me," she said, trying to sit up. "I'm...I'm perfectly fine." However, she needed her husband's arm to stand up and make her way down to the lobby. Oscar Leland sidled his way through the crowd towards them. "Did you like the show? Unfortunately, I can't take you to meet Count Belinsky after all. He won't see anyone tonight. 'I have nothing left to give'—that's just what he said. I pleaded, but he almost threw me out. You know how it is with artistic temperaments."

Mrs. Aylesworth held an evening of whist, three tables with the players moving from one table to the next. As usual, Margaret had to whisper several names to Henry, who had forgotten them: Mr. and Mrs. Field, Barnabas Rosebottom, the spinster Miss Cummings, Reverend Halliwell. He was glad that Margaret had Althea Beachcroft to exchange glances with, for he knew that she did not care for Mrs. Aylesworth's pretensions. He himself joined the card players reluctantly; he played all games poorly because he did not pay sufficient attention, a trait that Margaret claimed had endeared him to her.

After the last hand, they went into the drawing-room, which Mrs. Aylesworth had decorated in Moorish fashion, with Turkey carpets, embroidered pillows, an enormous double-pouffe ottoman, and brass peacocks standing by the tile fireplace. It was the most talked-of room in town, and entering it Henry hoped that Margaret did not think her own Japanese parlour a failure.

"Mrs. Church, could we impose on you to play something on the piano for us?" said Mrs. Aylesworth. "It would be such a delight."

"Perhaps your guests would prefer conversation."

But the others protested. Althea urged her too, whispering under her breath, "She's hoping you're out of practice." Henry knew that Margaret took no pleasure in performing for others, but she had no choice and so arranged herself at the piano and began. She had been playing only Debussy these last months and began the "Nocturnes," music that Henry could not make head or tail of. It seemed to him that she played well, even if she did look uncomfortable under the scrutiny of the others.

The little audience applauded. Henry could not help feeling proud of her. Miss Cummings said, "How wonderful. I felt a moment of absolute rapture." Their hostess called for the sweets to be brought in: Battenburg and Swiss cakes, strawberry ice, bonbons. The talk was of town politics and the excavations at Crete. He saw that Margaret held her plate in her lap but did not eat. Mrs. Aylesworth's butler appeared under the archway.

"Count Belinsky," the butler said.

"My apologies for being so late." The count strode brusquely into the room, marched up to Mrs. Aylesworth, and took her hand.

"Our honoured guest," she said, looking about the room to register the impression. The strongman wore a black dress coat and trousers, and a white waistcoat and cravat; his gloves, too, were white. The hostess rose and took him round to the others, her prize to show off for the evening.

"Mr. and Mrs. Church. May I present Count Belinsky."

"How pleasant to meet you. I believe that you have been to see my little theatrical."

"Yes," said Henry, "but how did you know?"

"I recognize you, of course. Let me think: the second box on the left, balcony row. I have heard of your fine bicycle factory, Mr. Church. It would be a great honour for me if you might have the time to give me a tour."

"Of course. Any day you like."

"Our Mr. Church is also an inventor of some renown," said Mrs. Aylesworth.

"You are making sport of me. In truth, I am no better than an amateur."

"But what is an amateur?" said Count Belinsky, turning

88

his eyes to Margaret for the first time. His gaze made her look down. "An amateur is a person who pursues knowledge only for love. *Seulement pour l'amour de la sagesse.* Is that not so?"

"It is a flattering way to describe failure," said Henry.

Mrs. Aylesworth said, "The count has taken up half the fourth floor of the Excelsior. It is unfortunate that our town does not have a first-rate establishment."

"Oh, but I have very simple tastes."

The Beachcrofts, already introduced, joined them. George said, "I dare say, Count Belinsky, you are the first count of any kind we've ever had in this town."

"In Russia there are many counts and nobody is impressed. I am not a rich count nor a powerful one, but just a count."

Again he looked at Margaret.

Mr. Rosebottom too came up, with Reverend Halliwell behind him. "Count Belinsky, we were just speaking of Sir Arthur Evans' extraordinary find. To think that he has uncovered the remains of the most ancient civilization yet discovered."

"Personally, I find it all very frightening," said Althea. "The world has become so topsy-turvy. One moment the scientists are telling us the sun moves in one direction, and the next day they declare it moves in the very opposite."

"Or not at all," remarked her husband.

"That is the nature of science," Henry said. "Each new discovery raises more questions than the discovery itself has answered. And so we are led slowly towards truth."

"Truth?" said the count. "Do you believe there is such a thing, Mr. Church? I do not call it that."

"What do you call it then?"

Margaret had not meant to speak. The count looked again at her and said, "I call it mystery."

"Very good," said Reverend Halliwell. "You have captured the spiritual essence that science itself cannot explain."

"Come, come," said George Beachcroft. "Here we are talking about something halfway around the world when what we really wish to do is ask Count Belinsky about his extraordinary performances. What I'd like to know is how you keep underwater so long."

"And those predictions," said Miss Cummings, who had also joined them. "I have heard that several people have been electrified by them."

"Mortified is what I heard," said George.

"What I would like to know," said Mr. Rosebottom, "is how you came up with your act in the first place. It's the most peculiar exhibition I've ever seen."

"Poor Count Belinsky can hardly breathe," said the hostess. "We've pinned you against the ottoman, I'm afraid. Please, sit down, Count. Won't everyone sit?"

Margaret was already in her chair. From his seat on the ottoman, the count was slightly turned away from her. Henry had to move to the other side of the room, on the loveseat next to Miss Cummings. He had spent considerable time mulling over the count's act and had determined that some of his feats were real but others were tricks. The lifting of the anvil had particularly occupied him until he had determined that a powerful electromagnet could have been placed underneath the stage. The anvil itself was likely hollow but with the magnet turned on it would have been impossible for any number of men to move it. With the magnet turned off, however, the count could pick it up alone. He regretted having refrained from telling Margaret about his deductions.

"At least I can tell you something of how my performances began," said the count. "You see, I was not a strong child. I did not begin to walk until I was almost three years old. Everyone worried that something was wrong with me, both physical and here"—he pointed to his shaven scalp. "I have three older sisters and my father had waited a long time for a son, so I was a great disappointment to him."

"But I'm sure that isn't true."

"But it was, Mrs. Aylesworth. There is a lake on our estate. When I turned five my father decided that I should learn to swim. Only I did not want to learn because I was afraid. As a child I was afraid of so many things. But my father would hear of none of it; he picked me up and threw me in. The first time, I almost drowned, and he had to jump in himself and pull me out. This did not stop my father. The next day he threw me in again. And the next, and the next."

"How brutal," said Miss Cummings. "To be firm is one thing, but that is simple cruelty."

"Yes, it was cruel, but I am glad that he did it. Eventually, I did learn to swim. And to hold my breath so that I could go down deep and not be seen by my father. I learned to stay down longer and longer. Although a clumsy boy on land, and no good at the games other boys played, I found myself to be light and swift in the lake. I grew to love the water and made of it a second home. And so it remains."

He ceased speaking and the others were silent. Then a noise: Margaret's plate slid from her lap and overturned on the rug. Henry, leaping from his seat, came to her side.

"Are you all right, Margaret?"

"Yes, yes. I am so sorry, Mrs. Aylesworth. I simply must have let go."

She shook her head at herself but did not seem otherwise embarrassed. Already the maid had arrived in the room to clean up, and the men were invited to try their hand in the billiards room, where they might smoke. Henry took Margaret's arm with a delicacy that seemed to irritate her.

He gave the count a complete tour of the building—forges, stamping machines, wheel assembly, chain-making, enamelling. The workers stared at the strongman as he paused to examine a labour-saving device or watched the moving line of bicycles hooked by their front wheels on the overhead chain conveyer. Even those who had not seen his show knew who he was. The count looked as if he might burst the seams of his neatly tailored jacket, while the collar of his shirt seemed about to spring loose under the pressure of his neck. The count admired and praised all that he saw. He voiced interest in every aspect of the business, not just manufacturing but distribution and promotion as well, and as Henry had just received the designs for their exhibit at the Toronto Industrial Exhibition in early September, he brought those out too and the count examined them closely. When they had seen the factory, he took his guest on a walk around the rows of workers' houses, the modern sanitation system, the community house.

"Our czar, who loves his people, would be most impressed by your paternal care," the count said.

Outside, they watched crates of finished bicycles being loaded onto a train pulled into the private siding. A team of four men pushed a crate up a ramp towards the open compartment. A wheel on the trolley snapped and the crate, tilting, began sliding sideways off the edge of the ramp. Even as the men were shouting, the count leapt forwards and lodged his shoulder under one corner of the crate. With a grunt he heaved it back onto the trolley, keeping a hand on it as the men pushed it the rest of the way into the train.

Afterwards, they went into Henry's office, where the count threw himself into an armchair and closed his eyes as if to nap. Henry did not know if he should say something or remain silent, but the count himself began to speak. "Mr. Church, you have a very impressive business here. Your machines are much more advanced than anything we have in Russia. We could not run such an operation there. It would be impossible."

He practically shouted the last word, opening his eyes again. "This is a very pleasant town. I need to remain somewhere awhile and work on a new act. Perhaps I shall stay here."

"I'm sure you will be most welcome."

"What is that book on your desk?" The count sat up, frowning. "Kropotkin?"

Henry reached to pick it up, but the count's hand got there first. The Russian let himself fall again into the chair as he opened the book.

"One of my workmen lent it to me."

The count sniffed loudly through his wide nostrils. "In Russia, we have extremists of many types. They try to force their way into history, to make great changes for the good of the people. The *good* of the people! Ha!"

"But surely there is some truth in their criticisms. In the injustices they point out."

"Of course. There is no perfect society. But they are fools to expect heaven on earth. They refuse to recognize human nature."

"I hardly understand them perfectly, but I believe they contend that the conditions of inequality are what distort our natures."

"My friend, society has not distorted anything. Society is a reflection of our nature. Humans are thinking beings, but they are not rational. In my opinion we are much closer to the wild animals than we pretend. These radicals are dangerous to our welfare—and the welfare of my czar. They are not so many, but they do not need to be. They have international connections, and a few can cause great upheaval and unhappiness." His voice rose and he slapped his hand on the book. "They do not respect borders, countries, property, or principles of decency. And what is the name of this studious workman of yours?"

"Giancarlo Caporale. Why do you ask?"

"It is only idle curiosity. And this conversation has turned rather glum." He looked at Henry and smiled humourlessly. "We should let others deal with these questions. I am merely a performer, and you—you are an inventor and a builder of bicycles. We have other ways to contribute, yes?"

A knock sounded on the door. Tyler, an unusually tall and lugubrious man who worked in the order office of Building Two, opened the door. "A message was just delivered, Mr. Church," he said. "From Mrs. Church."

Tyler handed Henry the letter and retreated. Annoyed to have to open it in front of the count, he roughly tore the envelope. *The Beachcrofts are dining with us tonight. Do ask Count Belinsky to join us.*

The count had closed his eyes again. His squat but muscular form looked as if it might splinter the chair he sat in.

"My wife requests that you dine with us this evening."

"Most delighted," the count said, without opening his eyes.

"I do not care for the opinions of our newspapers," said Mrs. Netherton, who had been invited to even the number at table. She had a faint moustache and several tufts of hair on her chin, which Henry tried to avoid staring at. "All this change is not for the better as far as I can see. It has increased ungodliness. It has made men arrogant and women forget their duties. The wireless. The automobile. Buildings six storeys high. Towers of Babylon, I say. And what will men do from these great heights? They will fire giant guns at one another, wreaking havoc and destruction. It will be the second Fall."

"Mrs. Netherton," said George Beachcroft, "you are a woman of great moral character. Your opinions can only influence those around you for the better. But surely there is some good achieved by these modern accomplishments. In medicine, for example. And what of greater prosperity. This is the beginning of a new era. Do you not agree, Count Belinsky?"

"Yes, with great enthusiasm. I believe in the future. I am a great admirer of the works of Jules Verne and H.G. Wells.

Imagine a ship to take us under the ocean. Or a machine that can transport us backwards or forwards in time. How astonishing that will be!"

"But that is make-believe," said Althea Beachcroft. "Mr. Church, you are our resident man of science. Do you not think so?"

He was folding his napkin in his lap, hoping to avoid having to speak. "I cannot say anything is impossible. A vessel that travels under the sea strikes me as feasible. But a time machine is a different matter. The past is gone and the future does not yet exist. How can we enter what is not?"

"And what is your opinion, Mrs. Church?" said Count Belinsky.

Margaret had been directing the serving of the consommé from a tureen on the sideboard. She looked at the count and then her husband. "I do not know. I think it is enough to try to live in the present."

"Yes, that is true enough."

"Speaking of scientific advances," said Althea, "you must tell us, Count Belinsky, about this photographic hobby of yours. My friend Doralene Rapp tells me that you have taken her photographic portrait. She says you have equipment of the highest quality, not like those new little boxes that everyone takes to the beach and so on. I also know— you mustn't deny it, Count—that Mrs. Rapp posed in the Elizabethan gown that she had made for the town costume ball last year. The one with the *décolletage*. Mr. Rapp did not want her to sit. Well, we all know how stuffy that man is, but in the end he gave in. Of course, she can't exactly put it over the mantel, can she, but Mrs. Rapp brought me into the bedroom to see it. And it is most remarkable. You have managed to make even Doralene Rapp look alluring, and that in my opinion shows unsurpassed talent. It does seem to me that with that little portrait by the bedside they will have to stop calling it the bedroom and begin calling it the *boudoir*."

"I hope the photograph is not actually compromising," said Mrs. Netherton, her soup spoon poised before her mouth.

The count smiled at her. "Mrs. Beachcroft tells a most amusing story, and I am delighted to be at the centre of it. But the photograph is in good taste, I assure you."

"Taste is a matter of opinion," said Althea. "I happen to be very liberal in these matters. Now tell us, dear Count, whether it is true that the mayor's wife is having hers done next, and she's having an Elizabethan dress especially made since she couldn't come to the ball last year, being in confinement."

"She has been very kind to agree to pose."

"But why haven't you asked me? I might agree too."

"Pardon me, Count," said George Beachcroft. "But you ain't taking my wife's picture without me in the room."

"Oh, you spoil all the fun."

"That is precisely what husbands are for, my dear."

The soup dishes were removed, and the pâté à la gelée brought in. "You must tell us how you take such exquisite portraits," said Althea. "So many that I have seen are just too awful. They make one long for the day when we could count on painters to make us look better than ourselves."

Margaret said, "Our friend will not let the conversation move on until she has satisfaction."

"Well, I don't see the use of skipping from subject to subject without finishing anything."

"There is no magic secret," the count said. "I simply get to know my subject before I take the photograph. I must have a feeling for the real person. Who she is and also who she imagines herself to be."

"That sounds a little dangerous," said George. "Don't you think so, Henry?"

"I have not considered the matter."

The count laughed. "It is not dangerous at all. We sit and have tea. We talk. And I learn from what is said and what is not. I use—ah, this is a word I don't know in English."

"Intuition," Margaret ventured.

"Perhaps that is it, yes. Intuition of the soul."

"Oh, you mustn't speak of souls," said Althea. "Mr. Church doesn't believe in them. He has banished them from the house."

"Now Mrs. Beachcroft, that isn't exactly the case—"

"I don't wonder that there *is* a danger," George said seriously. "Not of souls, but of pride. After all, don't women wish to appear beautiful and mysterious, and men handsome and powerful? The photograph is an invention of great utility. But to turn it into a romantic instrument— well, it's like Narcissus staring into the lake, what? We might fall in love with our own image. Myself excluded, of course, since I am far too ugly."

"Mr. Beachcroft," said his wife, "you ought not to attempt to sound clever. In my opinion, there is far too little romance left in this modern age of ours. But there is something else I want to ask you about your photographs, Count Belinsky. The one I saw of Doralene Rapp is so very small. I do not understand mechanical things but I do know that cameras can take much larger photographs."

"That is true, but my preference is for small ones. Perhaps it is because I possess a miniature portrait of my own mother, painted on ivory, in a small gold case. Such miniatures were intended as private keepsakes, and so I see my photographs. They must be examined closely, held in the hand in an intimate manner. They are not for display to the general public but for private contemplation by those most close to us."

The main dishes arrived: crown roast of pork, salmon à la Montpellier. More wine was poured from the decanters. The count swallowed half a glass and motioned for it to be refilled. He said, "Before my first camera, I tried to paint portraits. Well, I was not very good. One summer when I was sixteen I worked for weeks on a portrait of my second cousin, a girl one year older, whose name was Zinaida. She had come to stay with us for the spring and summer. Thin, pale, much more quick-witted than I was. Temperamental."

"You must have fallen in love with her," said Althea.

"Of course. I could not sleep at night. I wrote very bad poems. I offered her fervent gazes. Sometimes we went for rides in our small boat or for picnics. Once she allowed me to kiss her hand."

"I see an unhappy end coming," George said.

The count nodded. "I did not like my father's attitude towards her. He treated Zinaida flippantly, teasing her as if she were a child and not a woman. When she tried to speak of serious subjects my father would be sarcastic and even cruel. Once she actually ran crying from the room. Well, one morning in late summer I awoke at dawn. Something was making me uneasy. I rose from bed and looked out the window, from which I could see the back garden and beyond the fields of cherry trees. A figure was moving in the shadows of the garden. I knew immediately that it was Zinaida. Could she too not sleep? Perhaps she was even thinking of me. I was about to run down to meet her when I stopped. Another figure had appeared. The figure approached and Zinaida ran up to him and into his arms. I saw that it was my father."

"What a blackguard," George said.

"The rest of the day I sobbed like a child. As soon as I could, I slipped out of the house and took a horse from the stable to ride off into the fields, intending never to return. But at nightfall I was exhausted and hungry and I came back on my own. My father did not beat me as I expected but allowed me to confine myself to my room. Two days later Zinaida left for home. I never saw her again and my father and I never spoke of the matter. Now he has been dead ten years."

Silence. They resumed their eating. Henry said, "I would like to have a photographic portrait of Mrs. Church."

"Mr. Church," Althea laughed, "you come up with ideas at the oddest times. But it's true, Margaret, you would make a beautiful subject."

"It is a peculiar truth," said the count, "that the more beautiful the woman, the more difficult a subject she is to capture. Perhaps her beauty hides the deeper truth of who she is. But I would be most honoured to try."

Everyone had turned to look at Margaret. She had been looking at her plate, but now she forced herself to look up. "I am really too busy. My father has agreed to build a Sunday school for the children of the factory workers, and I am on the committee."

"But I am not leaving yet, Mrs. Church. Indeed, I have decided to spend the rest of the summer and early fall here while I develop my next show."

"How fortunate for us all, Count Belinsky," said Mrs. Aylesworth.

"But I still wouldn't like to sit for a portrait," said Margaret. "So there's an end to it."

"But that is good, not to be so eager," the count said. "That is very good."

Her screams were wordless, her body a vessel almost too frail to contain them. She shook, writhed, convulsed. He had tied her lower half to the bed but her upper body rose and slammed back again. Her arm flew outwards, cracking him across the lower jaw. As he moved aside, the same hand knocked Doctor Walsh's medicines off the side table, smashing them against the near wall.

"Hold . . . hold me . . ."

He grasped her burning body in his arms. Her own held to him tightly.

"I see . . . I see my mother."

"It is just the pain, darling."

"My mother. Oh God, she is sinking deeper and deeper. White. Her skin is white. And the water is so cold, so cold."

"You are with me, Margaret. In your own house."

"So cold. And so dark. And I am sinking too, into the dark, dark water. And, oh—I cannot breathe."

"Yes, you can, Meg. Just hold onto me."

"I am going to die, I am going to die! My lungs, they hurt so from the sting of the water. I don't want to die."

She rocked back and forth in his arms with such force that he could not keep her still but had to let himself move with her. Her fists were clenched against his back, her breathing desperately rapid.

"Mother, mother." Her voice was a searing whisper. "Such kind eyes and flowing hair. I am scared. You smile, but so sad you are. Why are you sorry, Mother? Where do you have to return? Do not swim away, let me come with you, do not leave me ..."

She grew limp. Her head lolled backwards as he eased her onto the pillow. Pressing his ear to her chest, he heard her ragged breathing. "Meg," he said, but she did not answer. How quickly the episode had come on. He had hoped that they were gone forever and now this one, more severe than ever. He got up to fetch the damp cloth from a bowl on the dresser and wipe her perspiring brow. There had been too much excitement. She needed quiet above all. He would not sleep nor leave her bedside until morning.

He rode out at dusk with a single-barrel shotgun and a canvas bag slung behind him, up the dusty farm road to the edge of the wood. Dismounting, he led the horse along the old Indian trail. The waxing moon was still big and made the branches crossing the path easy to see, and it took less than an hour to reach the outcrop of rock on the rising land that thinned out the trees for a quarter mile or so. Henry tied up the horse so that it would not bolt if startled and walked to a natural blind of scrub bush at the outcrop's edge.

He loaded the shotgun and laid it on his lap to wait.

Two days ago he had spotted a Richardson's owl, and yesterday another, rarely seen around here. An example for his private study, to compare with the saw-whet he had in captivity, it would clarify some points of difference that had been debated in the local ornithological society journals. He could not deny a general falling-off of his interests lately, nor that he had to force himself to come out here, but he believed it would do him some good to place his attention on the larger world. Two other birds of prey appeared in the air over the outcrop, hunting for mice and voles. They dived and caught their prey and took off with them. It was a long stretch of waiting, his knees growing cramped, before the Richardson's owl emerged. It was small but mature in its markings, and it took up a position near the top of a white pine, almost on the other side of the outcrop, too far for an accurate shot. He kept the shotgun on his lap, knowing that if he raised it to his shoulder he would tire before a good chance came.

A quarter of an hour passed. The owl did not move.

Henry grew drowsy. His sleep had been fitful lately. Perhaps that was why new ideas for inventions had not been coming to him. The owl swooped down, scrabbling its claws along the granite before rising again. It landed on a lower branch in a tree closer to Henry's side. He could see that its claws were empty. Slowly he raised the shotgun and sighted down the barrel. Still far, but he was a good shot. He felt some reluctance, for it was a beautiful creature, as all birds were, and he had killed enough to know how different they looked when the spirit had fled them. He pulled. The gun recoiled against his shoulder. The owl blew backwards off the branch, wings unfolding like a pair of fans. He could hear it land with a soft thud. Henry had to make himself get up. He went over with the gun and the bag and checked to make sure the bird was dead. Then he wrapped it in several rags and placed it in the bag.

The long trek back to the house seemed to take ages in the dark of the woods, the horse reluctant to set its hooves down on the trail. But at the moon-bright road he mounted again, and the horse broke into a canter. When they reached the path to the house, he reined in so as not to arouse the household.

He woke the boy to brush down and feed the horse in the stable and took a kerosene lamp out to the shed by the aviaries. After gutting the owl, he hung it from a rafter to dry out. He watched the birds for a time before going quietly into the house, avoiding the bedroom where Margaret had been sleeping for two hours already, and climbing to the turret instead.

That big moon loomed in the turret's open window. It made the grass and the willows along the river shine in silver outline. A slight breeze, warm on his face. He had saved a letter from Chester and now picked it up, using a knife to slit it open. Chester's characteristic scrawl sloping down the page. Looking up a moment, he saw something flash in the river between the trees. But he could see nothing more and returned to the letter.

Now that you are coming to Toronto for the Exhibition you have no excuse not to attend one of the meetings of the club. If nothing else, you will be amused to discover that there are men whose inventions are even less practical than your own. Perhaps you might even present a paper. There are some good people here too,

with sharp minds and generous of praise. And, of course, I look
forwards to seeing you, for it has been too long, Henry.
Sometimes I think you are a reluctant friend, or simply prefer
the company of birds and bicycles to humans…

That flash again in the river, catching the corner of his
eye. He still could not see what it was, so he rose from
his chair to fetch the field glasses from the cabinet. Standing
before the open window, he raised the glasses and gave his
eyes a moment to adjust. Saw the willow branches clearly
dangling. Focusing past them, he saw the river, reflective as
black glass. A movement crossed his vision but he lost it
and scanned the water without success. There again—a
swimmer's arm breaking the surface and falling again. He
kept absolutely still, only swivelling the glasses, trying to
estimate where the swimmer might come up again.

The water breaking, hair tossed, bare shoulders. And he
saw that it was Margaret, as he knew it had to be. Though
she had promised not to swim at night any more.

He watched her as she half rose out of the water, her
breasts glistening, then turned over and swam on her back
with leisurely strokes, keeping her lower body just under
the surface. He lost her behind a willow and found her a little farther on, although if she went much farther the river
would bend out of sight. She tilted her face up to the
moon, letting her dripping hair fall back. He became conscious of his own arousal, pressed against his trousers. At
the farthest reach of his sight, she suddenly submerged and
he could not make her out again.

Perhaps he could see better if he turned off the lamp on
the desk; lunging towards it, he cracked his shin on a drawer.

In darkness himself now, he looked along the length of the river. Yes, there she was again, by the rock that the locals called Gibraltar. Grasping onto it, she pulled herself up out of the water: shoulders, breasts, waist, belly, just to her navel, before letting go and sinking again. Something splashed next to her; he thought he glimpsed a fin. A fish had jumped, remarkably close to her. He shifted his stance. And saw something else.

On the far bank of the river, a figure in the darkness of the trees.

He shifted the glasses again to be sure that Margaret was still by the rock and then swung back to the trees. Nothing. A feeling of alarm rose in him, but he resisted the impulse to drop the glasses and rush down the stairs and out of the house to the river. He would wait one more moment as he scanned the opposite bank. Yes—there. The figure again, a dark form only, but clearly looking down at the water. Henry searched for Margaret, but she was no longer by the rock. He picked her up swimming back towards the shore. After a few strokes his view of her became obscured by the rise of the near bank.

Back to the figure; he had taken several steps forwards and was at the crest of the opposite bank, one hand on a tree trunk for balance. Whoever he was, he could see Margaret as Henry could not. There was a pause of ten or twenty seconds before she appeared, running up the lawn, clutching her silk robe to herself.

FALL 1900

*F*rom the train he could see the lake-crossing steamships in the Toronto harbour, the lumber and brick depots along the rail yards, the iron foundries, the furniture manufactures, the machine works. The factory windows were filmed with soot, and the smokestacks spewed ashy smoke into the wan sky. A worker in the coal yard leaned on his shovel, gazing dully at the slowing train. A piercing whistle. They halted at the station platform—he had forgotten the city could be so crowded—and a porter took his club bag, a handsome work of olive pebble leather Margaret had given him for his last birthday, and hailed a cab from the row of drivers on Front Street.

It was an open cab, and he swayed as the horse drew them along Front. He saw men in bowlers and soft hats with wide brims, women in walking skirts that left their boots visible. Boys hawking newspapers or sitting on their shoeshine boxes and spitting tobacco into the gutter. The electrical cables overhead felt to him like a net cast over the street. They passed cast-iron ware rooms, fancy goods shops with plate-glass windows, brick buildings five storeys tall. The cab turned up Church Street, pulled past St. James Cathedral and on to his hotel.

He always stayed at the Elliott House, an elegant corner building with a mansard roof. The cabman brought down his bag and the hotel porter took it inside, Henry following past the dark carpets and deep chairs to sign the guest register. He climbed the stairs to the third floor, found a coin for the porter's open hand, and was alone in his room.

The open window looked upon a lawn, but the grating noises of the city drifted in. He lay on the bed without taking off his shoes. He could imagine lying here and never getting up again. On the night before his departure, he had attempted to make love to his wife. She had lain in bed, unresponsive but acquiescent, the way Henry had assumed a woman would act before he married Margaret and discovered how thrillingly different she was. Last night she had merely stared at the wall, making him feel a kind of dark terror. He himself could not be aroused. She had been surprised, had even made an attempt to excite him by running her hands over his body, but she kept her face turned away and he was flooded not with terror now but with emptiness and grief.

A shame that he could not have described had sickened him. After she was asleep he had lain there, wanting to wake her, to weep against her shoulder, but not moving.

The Industrial Exhibition had opened yesterday; he was expected any moment. His bag was still unpacked. The street noises grew louder. He did not move.

He did not like the hordes of people swarming into Machinery Hall and the Manufacturer's Building, crowding the entrances of the Crystal Palace. He had tried to get a cup of tea at the ladies' temperance booth but the queue had been too long and he had settled for a dirty tin cup at a wooden stand, where the man had offered to put in a shot of "hard stuff" for an additional fifty cents. A band of midgets dressed as clowns noisily parted the crowd, honking horns and handing out leaflets advertising a recreation of the Trojan War on the race track, with a hundred vessels on an artificial lake, a giant wooden horse concealing

109

dozens of handsome Greek warriors, actual catapults, and a Miss Ethel McGreavy, voted Toronto's Most Beautiful Girl, wearing an authentic, diaphanous Greek gown in her impersonation of the unfortunate Helen.

He dutifully visited the tents and booths of other proprietors: Imperial Cheese, Lever Brothers. This year the mode was to build enormous pyramids of products, ten and fifteen feet tall, and ask bystanders to guess how many boxes had been used. A man selling tins of shoe blacking had actually addressed him as "Friend." Nearby a woman began shrieking; her handbag had been cut away from her, leaving only the dangling strap on her arm.

This year, instead of a booth, the Dawes Bicycle Manufactury had its own tent near the Liberal Arts Building—the decision had been his father-in-law's—decorated with flags and banners. DAWES BICYCLES ARE THE SAFEST ON THE MARKET. STURDY YET REMARKABLY LIGHT. A DAWES BICYCLE IS A THING OF BEAUTY. MODELS FOR MEN, WOMEN, AND CHILDREN. EQUIPPED WITH THE PATENTED DAWES QUICK-TOUCH BRAKING SYSTEM. SEE OUR NEW LINE OF ACCESSORIES, HORNS, BASKETS. FREE LESSON WITH EVERY PURCHASE OF A NEW MACHINE. OUR INSTRUCTORS CAN HAVE YOU RIDING IN HALF AN HOUR. EASIER TO MAINTAIN THAN A HORSE, QUIETER THAN A MOTOR CAR, CHEAPER THAN BOTH. COME IN TO REST YOUR FEET AND ENJOY OUR FIRST CLASS ENTERTAINMENT. Even with the surrounding noise he could hear a boisterous musical beat as he approached the open flap of the tent, where men in their Sunday clothes and women in white blouses and large hats were peering in. He hoped that meant that all the benches inside were full up, but he was disappointed on entering the relative gloom to see that fewer than half the seats were taken. At the back of the stage the various bicycle models revolved on a platform while, for no obvious reason, three men in blackface sang and played banjo and shuffled in front. The smell of the canvas conjured up a revival meeting or a circus. A pretty young woman handed him a sheet. He stared down at it. "The Dawes Two-Wheeler Waltz."

"Why, Mr. Church! We didn't expect you to just wander in like a customer. How do you like our show?"

He saw Jefferies, the Toronto store manager. Last year there had been a complaint about him getting fresh with a woman customer, but he had called it a misunderstanding. Henry said, "I don't quite see how a minstrel show is going to sell our bicycles."

"This is just to bring them in, Mr. Church. Get them to rest their sore dogs and enjoy themselves. After this the bikes come down. It's amazing the kind of fancy riding our boys can do on that little stage. And, of course, we've got the booth in the building next door. That's where we take the interested customers, give them the old Dawes Balance Examination. You should have seen me an hour ago, Mr. Church. Lady comes in with her daughter, wants the kid to take the test. So I give it to her and the kid scores high, naturally. But then I suggest that the mother try it. At first she doesn't want to, she's never even thought of riding one of those contraptions, as she calls it. All tittering laughter, won't stand on one foot, you know how it is. But I finally convince her and behold, wouldn't you know it but the mother scores even better than the daughter. I'm all amazement, of course, call over the other salesmen to look. Mr. Gordimer, he's a sharp new man, says that the only person who ever scored that high was Jack Rowe, fellow who won that race in Boston last year. Ten minutes later the woman was signing a cheque for a deluxe woman's touring model, and a kid's, too. Excuse me a minute, won't you, Mr. Church. I see a couple of good prospects near the front and better send a couple of our boys after them."

Henry was glad to be left alone. He listened another minute and then slipped back out of the tent. All of this— this noise and laughter and hucksterism—was the real, genuine world, where men survived or failed by their guile. Did he think he was too good for it, he who had been an orphan and charity case and might have ended up on the streets or worse if not for the patronage of Mr. Dawes? But he backed away from the tent, bumping shoulders with someone behind him and mumbling an apology even as he hurried on.

My Dearest Meg,

You would not like Toronto now any more than you have in the past. It is crowded for the Exhibition and not nearly as clean as its reputation has it. At the end of the day I must wipe the soot from my shoes. There are reports of confidence men selling cheap watches made up to look like gold to country visitors and using other methods to bilk them out of their money. And still the city feels just like a big provincial town, and without the sophistication that is the compensation of such a place.

I have now spent a considerable amount of time at our displays at the exhibition as well as at the ware room on King Street. In my opinion it looks better than any of the competition and your father's idea of creating a little "country path" in the store complete with bushes, gravel, and the sounds of birds has made an excellent effect. He is a natural salesman, your father, and I marvel at his particular genius. I'm afraid that I have come up with no new or novel ideas to offer, but I have at least tried to encourage our staff and make a good show of inspecting every detail.

Yet all of this is of minor interest. I would much rather receive a letter from you, dear Margaret, even if it were only a single sentence. How are you keeping busy? I have no doubt that you are making sure that James is taking care of the birds. Perhaps you have seen the Beachcrofts; please send them my best wishes.

I expect that some small amount of your time has been spent posing for Count Belinsky. It is most gratifying to me that you finally agreed to allow the Count to make one of his "miniature portraits" as he likes to call them. Of course it is inconvenient and perhaps even uncomfortable to subject oneself to the scrutiny of the camera. And yet the result is so very worthwhile, and I shall be most glad to possess such a photograph of you. In future I will be able to take it with me on my trips. Not that I expect it to assuage my loneliness for you and my yearning for your presence; if anything the likeness will only make them worse!

I will not bore you any longer. Please send me a telegram; it need not be long. Whatever shop window I pass, whenever a waiter speaks to me in a restaurant, even when I lie down at night, I think of you. There are so many things I cannot say, Margaret; they freeze on my lips. But I feel them every moment of every day.

Your devoted husband

In the back room of McConkey's Restaurant, the chairman of the Toronto Inventors' Club was banging his spoon on the table. Henry knew this Archibald Thrift only by reputation as a man who drank no spirits, coffee, tea, or even fruit juice, but only water that had been filtered through what he called the rejuvenating properties of asbestos. He had a monk's ring of white hair and wore the checkered suit of a travelling salesman. Among his inventions were the Thrift Automatic Self-Fingering Violin and the Thrift Rug Beating Machine. Chester Canty had introduced Henry upon their arrival to several others whose names he had already forgotten. Not surprisingly, they favoured eccentric dress and poor manners. One fellow had a small metal device attached to his cigar for catching the ashes, but every time he turned his head the ashes were dumped onto his green jacket.

Finally they settled down and turned their attention to Thrift. "Gentlemen of the Inventors' Club, let me welcome you to our monthly meeting. Gathered around this table I see some of the finest minds not only of this city but, I would venture to say, on this continent. You are not ordinary men. Of this none of you needs reassurance. While most of the great seething populace of our planet lives only for the moment, sees only the world in which he presently lives, imagining no other, you are different. Your eyes are turned to an inner vision. An inner vision that anticipates things to come. And that future will arrive because of that vision of yours.

"But it is not easy to be a visionary. We are often looked at askance by the rest of the population, by those without our imaginations. We are considered odd, even sometimes delirious or out of our minds."

"Speak for yourself, Thrift," someone shouted drunkenly.

"All right, Mr. Carlaw. Another word from you and I will remind everyone of the Carlaw Electric Hair Curling Helmet, which had to be removed from the marketplace after several unfortunate incidents and the settling of a half-dozen lawsuits. Let me continue. We are men not only of vision, then, but of courage. The courage to endure laughter, ridicule and dismissal, until finally our ideas are not only accepted but become so commonplace that our friends and neighbours can hardly remember a world without them."

"Move it on, Thrift," someone else called. "Or we'll invent a device for making you talk faster."

"Quiet! Well then, to our main speaker of the night. I believe that all of you know Mr. Bartholomew Rakes, proprietor of the Rakes Funeral Parlour in the village of Yorkville. Mr. Rakes has made some fascinating contributions to the field in which he toils on a daily basis, several of which he introduced first at one of our own meetings. Tonight Mr. Rakes will speak of a new process which he calls Electroplating the Dead—"

Henry tried to listen, but he found his mind unable to take in the words. Around him several men were making sketches of their own on the napkins or in notebooks. He himself had no ideas at all at the moment. Even among the peculiar, he did not seem to fit in. Or perhaps it was just that his mind kept returning to Margaret. Thinking of what she was doing at this very moment. Was she eating dinner and, if so, alone or with company? She might be reading a book. Or giving the raven a treat; she too had grown fond of the bird. It was difficult to have useful and practical thoughts when one was always thinking of one's wife.

When the meeting finally adjourned he and Chester slipped away and began to walk through the dark streets that had not yet been electrified. The younger Chester was not as tall as Henry, but he was broader and somewhat hulking in his walk. They came to St. James Cemetery and drifted along the winding paths and between gravestones and ornate tombs. The leaves rustled overhead. Henry found himself wanting yet unable to speak, and his friend, perhaps sensing the dilemma, also remained silent. In time they came to the small chapel, and when Chester tried the door it opened before them. Inside the room, with its low slanted ceiling, a candle burned on the altar, shedding a flickering and shadowy light.

"I wonder who left that for us."

"Chester, I think I am in difficulty."

"What sort of difficulty, Henry?"

"I do not know. Or I cannot say. It is Margaret. She is not what I have believed. And yet I don't understand why I believe—why I *know* this."

His words choked him. He sat on a bench and put his hands over his face. Although he could not look at his friend, he could hear Chester's pacing back and forth on the stone floor.

"Of course, Henry, I cannot understand precisely what you mean. But I do not have to. I see that something serious is happening to you, an experience that you yourself cannot explain. I know Margaret to be greatly devoted to you."

"Yes, yes."

"People do change, Henry. Some more than others. Or they become more themselves, what they did not recognize themselves to be. But I also must ask whether you are in fact feeling a change within yourself? Perhaps you are afraid of some personal truth and so must pretend that it is Margaret who is different. I suggest this, dear friend, only because I know this fear myself only too well."

"I cannot breathe in here."

"I will accompany you back to your hotel."

Again they walked in silence. The taverns had already closed and the streets were empty. Occasionally a carriage drove by with its curtains drawn. Finally Henry said, "You spoke before of your own fear."

"It is of no matter."

"I am your friend too, Chester."

"Yes, but I have no need to speak of it."

"Perhaps your experience will be of use to me."

"That I do not know. And there is always the risk that it may turn you against me. I would not like to lose you, Henry. Although we don't see one another often, you are important to me."

"And you to me. So that could never happen."

He could hear Chester's breathing. "Very well, then. I am one who loves men rather than women."

"You are a sodomite?"

Chester laughed sharply. "That is not the word I would use. Homophile is more to my liking. Like the Greeks we used to read together. Like Mr. Wilde, languishing in prison."

Henry had stopped walking. Chester turned to face him and Henry looked at his round, good, open face. He would not allow himself to turn away from his friend. He surprised himself by asking, "And is there a man with whom you—I don't even know how to say it."

A tuneless whistle made them both turn. A policeman was coming up the other side of the street, hands behind his back as he eyed them. "Let's keep walking," Chester said, and they fell into step together again. "This is a dreary city for one of my inclinations. Yes, Henry, there is a man I love now. A beautiful young man, whom I am tutoring in mathematics and Latin. But he lives in his mother's house and she is suspicious. If I am not careful, my heart will be the ruin of me. Now tell me more of your own troubles. Do you think I might be right? That you are the one who is changing?"

"I do not know."

They walked on, silent again.

He took breakfast as usual in the dining room of the Elliott House, where an efficient bustle of waiters marched in from behind the swinging doors of the kitchen and carried large trays over the heads of the guests. The businessmen all had their newspapers folded at their elbows and Henry too had his *Daily Mail*.

LECTURE SHOCKS AUDIENCE

Viennese Doctor Upsets Medical Establishment
Mrs. Horace Livermore Faints

A medical lecture on Thursday evening caused much consternation in the audience and caused at least one person to suffer fainting and palpitations. Doctor Karl Fruhauf of the University of Vienna, visiting Toronto as part of a tour of asylums for the insane in Canada and the United States, gave the lecture to an audience of lay persons and professionals in the main lecture hall of University College. Afterwards, many in the audience believed that the lecture, entitled 'Psycho-dynamic Origins of Male and Female Sexual Deviancy,' ought to have been restricted to members of the medical profession. The title of the lecture had not been announced beforehand.

Among the seventy or more attendees were not only such well-respected Toronto medical men as Doctors Oswald and Arshington, but also several dozen members of the city's better classes. Doctor Fruhauf remained composed, neither answering nor hesitating in his speech when members of the audience, forgoing the usual rules of etiquette, shouted at the speaker. Nor did he stop when Mrs. Horace Livermore fainted, creating a considerable disturbance in the back of the crowded hall as the insensible woman was carried out.

As for the content of the lecture, the editors of this newspaper doubt whether its readers would approve of more than a partial account. Suffice it to say that Doctor Fruhauf asserted that even respectable people had "desires that would be considered indecent when judged by present morality." Free will was an illusion because these impulses were not subject to the workings of the rational mind but came from "darker, more primitive, and as yet unknowable depths" that the new science was only beginning to investigate.

A faculty member of Vienna University, Doctor Fruhauf is currently residing at the Queen's Hotel. Despite the vocal denunciations, Doctor Fruhauf insisted that he would remain in the city for several more days in order to consult with colleagues and visit local institutions.

Was it the phrase "free will" that so caught his attention or simply the word "desire"? He had begun to read the account a second time, when a sound beyond the window attracted his attention. Outside, a hay cart had lost a wheel, tipping its load across Shuter Street and halting a funeral procession led by a black-plumed stallion. He went back to the article and considered taking it with him, but changed his mind and left the newspaper behind on the table. What he really wanted to spend his free time on was finding Margaret a gift, something unusual and precious, that would appeal to her elusive sensibility—an object to express both his adoration of her and his admiration for her individualism that would reveal how well he truly knew her and so reawaken her to his feelings.

He went into the shops on King Street and on Yonge, where he considered gloves and scarves and hats, silver-handled brushes and porcelain figures, paintings-on-glass, parasols, brooches and stick pins, finger purses and perfume bottles and chatelaine watches. But none remotely reflected his state of mind or exposed anything true about Margaret.

Although it was September, the day had that peculiar gritty warmth characteristic of the city. The shops felt airless, the fans turning overhead merely moving the warm air about. He had some trouble catching his breath, while increasing desperation propelled him into yet another store. But he found nothing, nothing, and he was on the sidewalk again, steadying himself against a lamppost and wiping his brow with a handkerchief.

When he took the handkerchief away from his eyes he saw, as if some act of conjuring had placed it there, a small bronze plaque on the street door in front of him.

Cripp's Museum of Natural,
Human and Inhuman Phenomena
All Exhibits Guaranteed Authentic
Entrance 25 cents

Beside the door was a window display being ignored by everyone else who passed by. He saw what looked like the skeleton of a gorilla or chimpanzee, with a top hat set on the skull at a jaunty angle and a cane wired into the curling fingers of one hand. A small electrical motor, not hidden but placed on a bit of old velvet, caused the skeleton hand to raise and lower the cane in a jerky manner. There was a "Chinaman's Opium Pipe," a row of shark's teeth, and a stuffed and mounted platypus. Hardly a serious museum, but he was glad to be taken out of his own thoughts for a few moments and found himself opening the door. He paid his coin to the young man drowsing with open mouth at the desk and went into the first room.

There were wooden cases with glass doors, not well made, and only a dim light overhead. He saw a handful of Egyptian scarabs, the horn of a rhinoceros, a display of mineral samples with their labels so faded as to be almost indecipherable. In the cases of the second room were large preservative jars, the formaldehyde gone cloudy but their contents still visible: a six-legged cat, a lamb with a second, smaller head next to the first, a stillborn human infant with a tail like a monkey. Then up the narrow stairs to another set of rooms, from the first of which came various scuffling noises. He found it lined with small cages on wooden stands, inside which were snakes, toads, a Mexican horned toad, rodents from South America, and a parrot huddled on its perch and with its tail feathers missing. When he put his finger to the cage, the parrot did not approach or even try to strike him, but buried its head further into itself.

In the next room the light had gone out, and he could see only by what illumination came in through the open doorway. Here, he thought, the animals were better off, being dead—stuffed and mounted in artificial positions meant to give them a menacing look. There were glass cases here too, containing an Indian headdress and German sabres, and, at the rear, in a separate case, was another mounted creature, hideous enough to draw him to it in spite of himself.

It had the head and body of some female apelike thing, a baboon perhaps, with shrivelled breasts, and a face grimacing as if it had died in excruciating pain. But its lower half was of some very large fish, the scales dried and flaking away, the fins turned black. Before it lay a small card; he had to bend down and almost press his face to the glass to read it in the near darkness.

The Feejee Mermaid
as presented by Mr. Phineas T. Barnum
in the Broadway Concert Hall, New York City, 1842,
to enormous crowds and considerable controversy

He stood up again. What controversy could there have been over such an abomination? True, the stitching had been done so cleverly as to be invisible, yet it was clearly a fabrication, a hoax. Such an animal could be no more real than a minotaur or sphinx. Next to it was an original handbill from the concert hall showing, with an engraving of a beautiful mermaid sunning herself on a rock. With flowing hair and bare breasts, her tail turned up out of the water, she gazed at her own reflection in a hand mirror. So people had expected to see some alluring creature and instead were repulsed by a haglike monstrosity. It was too ridiculous. And yet his eyes were drawn again, not to the thing in the case, but to the image in the engraving.

He heard something. Quick footsteps, a rustling of material, a breath taken in, and then full darkness as someone closed the door. He held himself still.

"I told you this room was quiet as a church." A male whisper. He thought it was the same man who had taken his money. "Just some animals as ain't going to mind. Come here, then."

"Quit your fooling." A woman. "I don't like it in here, it gives me the willies. What if somebody comes up?"

"They can't come up if they can't buy a ticket now, can they?"

"But you said someone already come in today."

"He left when I went to the back room. Nobody stays longer 'en half an hour. Ah, but you got a nice shape, Elsie."

"Watch those hands now." Laughing. "You sure no one can come in?"

"If they try I'll sic the old stuffed bear on him. Aarr!"

The man's growl turned into the sound of nuzzling. Shifting and pulling of clothes. Muttered half-words and moans and then quickened breaths. A wooden case began to rock against the wall. And Henry, trapped here, as if to be tormented and ridiculed. He felt his face burn, his groin burn, anguish swell in him.

Dearest Margaret,

Tomorrow is my last obligation at the Exhibition, and the next day I will be home. Only one brief telegram from you, but no matter now that I will soon return. How I long to be home—to my house, my birds, and to you. Dear Meg, some thoughts have been occupying me the last days, and in truth I have been thinking of little else. Despite the most frank and intimate relations, it can sometimes be difficult to speak what is most pressing on one's heart. And so I write this letter and hope that inspiration can bring me the words I need.

Beloved, you have grown distant in recent months. Even when we are together, sitting over breakfast or taking an evening stroll, I often sense that you are holding back something, as if not allowing yourself to be fully in my company. Also, you are sometimes short-tempered and irritable. Of course, I provoke you with my absentmindedness and other faults, and every day I berate myself for them and struggle to improve myself. But it is also true that in the past you were more forgiving of them. And now I feel that, despite what I believe are honest efforts to be a husband worthy of your respect and love, in your eyes I fail a little more with each passing day.

I understand that relations in a marriage change over time. I do not expect you to look upon me as you once did, or wish for my company with the same urgency, or feel, as you whispered on our first night together, that you cannot imagine living without me. I would settle for a quieter, more mature affection, and if I felt that this was the direction in which your own feelings were moving I would say no more. But instead, dear Meg, I feel that you have chosen to close your heart from me. Am I dreaming this? Am I simply a fool, a husband past thirty, married five years, yet still with a young man's infatuation for his bride? I write this letter not to seek explanations, or to force from you expressions of affection that you cannot or wish not to provide of your own free will. But I do write to make my own feelings vivid to you again in the hope, the desperate hope that by some miracle your own may reawaken. And so I write to say that I love you most dearly, that no other woman could mean the same to me, that my life and my fate are bound to you.

Knowing you and your goodness, I cannot but think that you also must be suffering, but in a manner that is unknown to me. What else could take you from me in this way? I want to believe that I can help, can be a source of relief and happiness to you, and by so doing bring you back to me. I will not write again before I return on the afternoon train in two days. Do not come to the station; I wish to see you at the house. Our house.

All I wish for in this life is to regain your love.

Your devoted husband

After breakfast there was still more time to waste before he needed to arrive at the Dawes' exhibition tent, and so he left the hotel and began to walk without purpose. He wandered distractedly for some time and found himself in what must have been a street in St. John's Ward: narrow houses backed by tarpaper summer kitchens. In back gardens as small and square as handkerchiefs he saw a few lettuces and beans gone to seed, a chicken scratching in a coop made from a broken chest of drawers, piles of ash and broken crockery. Odour of boiling vegetables. Inside one of the houses a child was crying while an adult shouted. In a kitchen doorway a man in a dirty jacket stood smoking.

He walked to the end of the alley and turned the corner. Here was a small shop, inhabiting the front room of a house, a wooden sign suspended by an iron bracket over the door. "Mrs. Pankhurst's Shop of Curiosities." In the window was a good deal of cheap jewellery, some old maps, a violin, a cast-iron penny bank in the shape of a turbaned Indian sitting on a tiger. It seemed an unlikely place to find a gift for Margaret, but he had so far failed to find anything special in the better shops, and so he went up the dilapidated stairs and through the curtain of hanging beads. The room, which had once been a small front parlour, was jammed with enough furnishings for twenty rooms: rocking chairs, commodes, and baby cots, and piled upon them smaller items—clocks and lamps, decanters with their stoppers missing, leather picture frames, military medals. On the walls, darkened from the soot of the old coal stove, hung snowshoes, paintings, a stuffed crocodile with a rubber boot in its mouth, a mandolin. The former possessions of the ruined and the dead. To even think of looking for a present here was an insult to his Margaret. He turned to go.

"Good afternoon, sir. May I be of assistance?"

He turned back again and saw an elderly woman in widow's dress, fleshy and blotched of face. A watering eye.

"Thank you, madame, I don't think so." He tipped his hat and began to move on.

"We have many interesting items not on general display. Perhaps you are looking for something special. A gift?"

"Well, yes. For my wife."

"If you would be so kind as to tell me something of her taste."

"That is not easy to say. She is unconventional. She does

not take to the usual things that women like. She does not collect. She is fond of music, however. And ... water."

"Yes?"

"Well, fond and afraid both, I think. We speak of voyaging across the ocean but always put it off." He did not know why he was telling this to a stranger.

"Then you must take her. Or bring the ocean to her. I have something that might catch her fancy. It is uncommon and so rather expensive, as might be expected. I purchased it from the captain of a vessel in harbour some three months ago but have yet to show it to anyone."

He took a step forwards. "May I see it?"

The woman half closed one eye and stared with the other, as if scrutinizing him for worthiness. As he waited for her to answer, he realized that he was holding his breath.

"One moment, if you will."

She turned around and, drawing out a ring of keys from the wide pocket of her skirt, unlocked a cabinet drawer. She drew out something—a narrow inlaid box some ten inches long—and held it out towards him. "Yes," she said again, "uncommon and expensive both."

He took the box and lifted the hinged lid. Inside, on a velvet bed, was a string of black pearls. Even in the poor gaslight of the shop they glowed with a dark luminescence he had never seen before.

"I have heard of black pearls but I did not know they really existed."

"They are rare, of course, and found almost nowhere but in the Gulf of Mexico. The pearl divers must be able to stay under for a terrible number of minutes to reach the oysters and cut them loose. I have only seen two other such necklaces in the last forty years, but neither was as fine as this one."

He raised them carefully from the box. "They are so precisely what I have been looking for that I cannot but feel a genuine gratitude to you, madame."

"In truth, I was not sure I wanted to sell them at all. But I have a soft heart and can see by your face all that they mean to you. The price is five hundred dollars. In banknotes."

"It is a good thing I went to the bank yesterday, Mrs. Pankhurst."

The woman cackled. "Pankhurst? I am not Mrs. Pankhurst. Nor Mr. Pankhurst neither. The both of them died one night, although which one tied up the other and then started the fire never did get settled for sure. I couldn't be bothered to change the sign. Now would you like me to wrap that up for you, sir?"

He was all impatience, waiting at the teller's window, his porter standing to the side with his bag. The large and flustered woman in a travelling suit before him was searching through her handbag for her money. Most likely she had never bought a ticket for herself before, but still he could not help tapping his foot and crossing and uncrossing his arms. At last she thanked the teller profusely, gathered up her things, and moved aside.

He asked for a first-class ticket, his voice sounding to him as if it came from someone else.

"I'm sorry, sir. The first train's been cancelled. Trouble with the boiler. It'll have to be the eleven o'clock."

"But that is impossible. I am expected home."

"The company does apologize for the inconvenience, sir."

"Yes, all right."

The idea of a three-hour wait seemed worse than intolerable to him. It meant almost six hours before he saw Margaret. What could he possibly do with himself? He had already had a last dinner with Chester and he had no desire to return to the bicycle shop.

He turned to the porter. "Hang on to my bag, will you? And meet me at the train."

"As you wish, sir."

A quick walk out of the station to the cab stand. "The Queen's Hotel," he said before mounting the step. It was a closed cab, and he was glad to be moving privately through the streets, feeling as if he had lost control over his own actions, as if some power were compelling him senselessly forwards. The cab pulled up to the hotel, which was substantially larger than his own, and he paid the fare and went through the doors and straight to the desk clerk.

"Can you tell me if Doctor Fruhauf is in?"

The clerk consulted the volume open before him. "I believe so. But he is due to check out any time. His bags have been sent for. Room 411."

The operator in the elevator cage took him to the fourth floor, pulling the iron grating open with an agonizing slowness. He had to restrain himself from sprinting down the hall until he found the door, upon which he knocked too loudly.

The door opened, revealing the suspicious face of a small man with a pointed beard. He wore a travelling cloak and a Homburg and a lorgnette balanced on his nose. "Yes? You have not come for the bags?"

"Doctor Fruhauf, my name is Edward Fetherling." He had rehearsed the name while in the cab. "I was hoping to have a word with you."

"My driver will be here any minute. I have hired a motor car."

"I promise to be brief."

"All right. Come in."

It was a small room. He motioned for Henry to sit down in one of the two armchairs at the foot of the bed. "No doubt you have a problem of a personal nature and wish to consult me."

"I would be very glad to pay your consultation fee."

The doctor's face registered displeasure. "Every city I visit has someone like yourself who appears at my door. Sometimes several. In Chicago two men got into a heated argument over who arrived first and resorted to fisticuffs. They all think I can analyze them and suggest a cure in ten minutes. None of them understands this new science."

Henry did not know what to say. The doctor had exposed his own foolishness; he had been hoping for just such a miracle cure.

"Ach, it is no matter. Please tell me what is troubling you."

"I find it hard to talk about, Doctor."

"Naturally." Not quite concealed impatience.

"I have been married for five years. But just lately there have been difficulties. And recently I did not succeed in ... in fulfilling my marital duties."

"Impotence."

"Yes."

"You would be surprised how common this is. I must ask you when was the last time you succeeded in fulfilling your marital obligations. Please remember that without absolute truth, our conversation can have no value."

"I understand. About three weeks ago."

"And when was your last emission?"

"Perhaps a week after that."

"But not with your wife?"

"No, alone. But after I had seen her undress."

"I see. It is so much safer to watch, isn't it? Like the little boy watching his mother perhaps. Tell me, was your marriage an arrangement of convenience or love?"

"For my part it was love. And for hers too, I know it."

"Yes, this is the irony. Such matches often cause the greatest mental suffering because so much more is expected. Tell me, when you attempted the act of sexual intercourse, what is it that you saw? In your mind, I mean. The image that came to you, perhaps when you closed your eyes."

"I do not understand how you should know to ask me that."

"Answer the question, if you would."

"I saw, I saw ... a beast."

"Hmm."

"Not a terrible beast or monster. I don't know how to describe it exactly. A beautiful beast but one that was wild and dangerous nonetheless."

A knock sounded on the door and the porter entered. Henry felt himself blush and he turned his face away, although there was no chance a porter would recognize him. The doctor nodded towards the remaining bags and the porter picked them up and retreated again. "I really must go or I will miss my next speaking engagement," said Doctor Fruhauf. "Unfortunately, Mr. Fetherling, we are taught a harmful lie from a young age—that women are delicate and fragile creatures requiring our protection and patronage. But the truth is that they are strong, perhaps stronger than us men. They have a force within them that is as old as life itself. Your unconscious mind understands this and your conscious self fears it. Only when you overcome this fear will your difficulties end. Now I really must go. Good day to you."

The doctor touched his Homburg as if to be sure it was still there, made a sharp movement of his neat head, and strode out of the room.

On the train home Henry could neither read nor write nor make easy conversation with the two other passengers in the compartment. When they got out at Berlin he was glad to be alone.

He walked to the dining car, drank a cup of coffee, walked back.

He took out the narrow box of pearls, wrapped in tissue and a ribbon. Fiddled with the ribbon until it somehow came untied, then quickly pulled off the tissue and opened the box. He was relieved to see the glowing black pearls still inside, as if they might somehow have vanished. He took them out carefully and touched their coolness to his face, then played with them by running the strand over the fingers of each hand in turn. Beyond the window, the trees had flared into autumn, so altering the appearance of the landscape that he might have been away for two months instead of two weeks. He set himself to thinking about all he had to do at home—reporting to his father-in-law, responding to the salesmen's suggestions to add a chain guard on the men's touring bicycle and to change the colour of the women's. He trusted that James had taken good enough care of the birds, but he would be satisfied only upon seeing them. And he must begin working on his inventions again; his mind had been bereft of new ideas during his entire stay in Toronto. And yet the conditions of city life offered far more opportunities for innovation than their own town. For example, what if one could devise a method for travelling from the roof of one five-storey building to another, eliminating the necessity of having to descend to the ground and cross the street? Say a chair, suspended on horizontal cables and worked by a pulley system run by the action of one's own feet.

He poured the pearls from one hand to the other before reluctantly putting them back in the box. Carefully, he folded the tissue and slipped the ribbon back on.

Although he had asked Margaret not to meet him at the station, and he was arriving on a later train, he was disappointed to find no one waiting for him. He pulled down his own bag and hired a cart to drive him to the house. Too anxious to sit in back, he swung up front next to the driver, whose long face Henry recognized from many years of working in the village. The man looked at him as if he were seeing an apparition and then said, "Mr. Church" in the most surprised and uncomfortable manner.

"Please take me home."

The man did not speak, but nodded. Nor did he say a word during the ride, just chewed his tobacco and spat over the side, so that there was only the sound of the horse breathing and its hooves clopping on the road. Henry strained forwards in his seat until the house came into view over the last hill: first the chimneys, then the turret, then the gabled main roof, and finally the rest of the house and grounds. It looked peaceful and handsome, with the trees in rust and the grass pale, and down by the water the willows drooping yellow. He could hardly contain himself—it *did* feel as if he had been away for years—and he had an urge to jump from the cart and run to the house like a boy. Someone was coming out—yes, it was Cook. She looked towards the cart and then went back in the house. A moment later she came out again with several others; more followed, the full household staff. He thought he glimpsed Margaret but could not be sure. Why did the damnable driver not get his horse to move quicker?

They came down the path to the front of the house, where the servants stood waiting in a row beneath the veranda. Margaret was not among them. He jumped down before the cart had stopped, almost falling to his knees but catching himself and coming up before them. None of them seemed to want to look directly at him. Margaret's maid, Mary, had a face inflamed, it looked as if from crying.

"What is it? What has happened? Mrs. Hendricks?"

The woman reluctantly looked at him. "One of the workers—what's his name, James?"

"Caporale."

"That's it. They found him dead this morning in the factory. Crushed by a stamping machine. Only it happened in the night and seemed so very unlikely. And there's something else as well."

"Yes?"

"I'm very sorry, Mr. Church."

"For God's sake, tell me."

"Mrs. Church is fled. With that Russian count. At day-break, and in a carriage with fast horses. I am very sorry, Mr. Church."

Days passed, he did not know how many. He neither shaved nor bathed nor changed his clothes. Trays of steaming meals appeared at the top of the turret stairs; twice he threw them back down, cups and bowls and dishes shattering, food splattering on the steps and rails and walls. No one dared to clean up.

The sounds that emerged from his own body were unrecognizable. Animal sounds, howls of primitive grief. He could barely see, his eyes stung so. After two sleepless nights, three, he curled up in a corner, slept, awoke before dawn, stared at the sky as it gradually lightened.

In the middle of the night, his insides began to tear themselves up. He vomited until his retches were dry, but the convulsions would not stop. He could not catch a breath and then, when he did, the stink of his own vomit made him start again. When finally he collapsed, his left temple struck against something. He felt it not as pain but as sound, an incessant jagged ringing in his skull.

The air so still he could hear the morning whistle at the piano factory. About the factory itself he cared nothing.

His legs trembling, he held the rail and took one step at a time past the encrusted remains of food he had thrown down centuries ago. In a storage cupboard he found a canvas bag to put his soiled clothes in and then turned on the bath and scrubbed himself until his skin was raw. Everything about his body was sore, his mouth was sour, his stomach felt as if it were feeding on itself. In the mirror he saw a face that was not his own: white and narrow, beard gone wild, a dark welt on the forehead in the shape of an isosceles triangle.

He dressed in trousers, shirt, waistcoat, tie, jacket, and went down to the ground floor, down the veranda steps, and straight to the aviaries. Unlatching the doors, he used a broom to chase out the birds. The handle felt unnaturally heavy in his hands, as if it were made of iron. Some of the birds refused to leave, scrambling everywhere but towards the open door, and it took him nearly an hour. Exhausted, he retreated back inside and lay fully clothed on the bed, while outside the trees were full of owls, falcons, pheasants, thrushes, all shrieking bloody murder.

On the twelfth day—it was James who informed him how much time had passed—it occurred to him to make enquiries. He thought of sending James to the coach and railway stations but could not bear the idea of someone else speaking her name aloud to another and the looks that might be exchanged. So he went himself, stopping at Margaret's davenport to write a note for James to deliver. His own last letter to her lay unopened. He dipped the pen and wrote:

Dear Mr. and Mrs. Beachcroft,

Can you tell me anything of Mrs. Church?

Respectfully,
Henry Church

He had no success at the railway station, but discovered that a coach had been hired by Count Belinsky, who had left after dark, accompanied by a woman whose face the driver had not seen. He had driven them through the night until they reached Toronto, where he had let them off at the Lakeview Hotel. They carried only two small bags.

On his return home there was a note waiting for him on the hall table. Quickly he tore it open.

Mr. Church,

Neither myself nor Mrs. Beachcroft know anything of Mrs. Church. Indeed, Mrs. Beachcroft is herself very distressed by recent events. As a result, I think it best if we do not have any correspondence with you at this time.

Yours,
George Beachcroft

He tossed the letter aside, his mind having already dismissed it. On his way home he had decided to search the house. He did not know what he expected or wanted to find, but he went through the bedroom, the dressing room, the parlours, the cabinets, bureaus, drawers. Margaret's davenport. But he found no letters or notes, no jewellery or other objects he did not recognize, which strangely disappointed him, as if he wanted to feed his despair with something actual, some tangible evidence. He called for James to bring down from the attic a small travelling trunk and for Mrs. Hendricks to make him coffee. He refused all help packing and knew the servants stood listening at the bottom of the stairs as he threw whatever of his clothing came to hand into the trunk. He was halfway through packing when he remembered the secret compartment in the davenport.

He sprinted to the small parlour. To reach the compartment he had to pull the davenport away from the wall, which he did so violently as to knock off a small Gall lamp, a wedding gift. He heard it crack but did not stop to look, feeling down the back of the davenport until he touched the recessed latch. The little door opened downwards and he reached in and grasped the object within.

It was a small album, bound in maroon leather. He stared at it in his hands for some time without opening it, trying to find its image in his memory even though he knew he had never seen it before. Then he sat on the edge of the damask seat of the davenport and opened the album.

To a small photograph of Margaret standing naked before a drapery. In her hands, just in front of her, she held a scarf or kerchief. He stared at the photograph, at her solemn face, her pale shoulders, her breasts with their dark aureoles, her navel, her hips, her legs, her feet turned out slightly. There was nothing seductive about the pose, not like the postcards available from under the counters of certain shops, yet that only made it more painful for him to see. Because she was so real, so much herself. And *he* had taken the photographs, that Russian, that circus performer. Why had she let him? A knife blade turned in his heart.

He turned quickly to the next: Margaret from the side, in the same place, still with the kerchief in her hands. The next: from behind, nothing hiding her here. The next—it was the last—from the other side. As if she were being photographed as a study in human form, or for medical reasons. He went back to the first, looked at them all again and again.

Mrs. Hendricks and James found him in the bedroom, beating himself with the buckle on his leather belt. They took it away, after which James led him compliantly to the bed and left him alone in the dark.

He awoke the following noon, washed and shaved, and allowed James to put ointment on the welts that had risen on his shoulders and back. He winced as the cambric of his shirt touched them, then continued to dress in travelling clothes. He completed the packing begun the day before, drinking the tea that Mrs. Hendricks brought up to him and eating two currant buns, wrapping a third in a napkin and putting it in his jacket pocket. The leather album he put into the trunk along with the box of black pearls before locking it shut.

The servants moved aside as he came down the stairs. He stood before them, not looking directly into any of their faces, but past them to the front door. He had difficulty finding his voice. "I wish the house to be shut up. Shutters bolted, furniture draped. I shall go to the bank in town and return with your wages and a month's bonus. I have already written letters of recommendation and have left them with Mrs. Hendricks. James, you are to sell the horses to Isaiah Marsh and deposit the money at the bank. For now, please have the trunk loaded onto the carriage and then take the reins. I wish to thank you all for your service."

Someone— it was Mary—began to weep. The stable-boy, twisting his cap, could not help grinning. Henry stepped by them and went directly out onto the veranda. At the end of the lawn a large pile of leaves was burning, the smoke rising straight upwards. The carriage was driven up and the trunk loaded onto the back. He would not look at the house. He took a deep breath and was about to step up into the carriage when a dark flash from the nearest tree drew his eye. The raven dropped to the slatted floor of the veranda. It pattered over to him, claws clicking on the wood. *Tuck, tuck, tuck.*

"Go away," Henry said. "You are free now."

The bird trilled and ruffled the feathers on its head. It waddled up and pulled at his shoelace.

"It's too late for you, is it? All right. Wait here."

But the raven followed him as he walked to the wooden shed behind the empty aviaries. From it he took a cage of brass wire. Then back to the house with the raven taking short flights behind. On the path by the carriage he put down the cage and, reaching into his jacket pocket, pulled out a piece of currant bun. The bird scampered towards him but stopped short. It tilted its head up and whistled. Took a small step. Another. Stretched out its neck. Henry grabbed with both hands. The raven brayed like a donkey, kicking out its feet but not striking him with its beak. He pushed the raven into the cage and closed the door.

Lifting the cage onto the carriage seat, he climbed in after. The servants had lined themselves up on the path, as they had on his return all those days ago. He looked quickly at them and then through the opposite window to the fire, the smoke growing heavier. A single burning leaf rose in the hot draft of air, somersaulting upwards for fifty feet and then sailing towards the river.

"Take me to the factory," Henry said.

He had the carriage drive through the factory grounds and out the back gate to the row houses behind. They were arranged in a square, with a central playing ground for the families. A few women were sitting on benches while their children played on the brown grass. They stopped speaking and turned to watch as he descended from the carriage and walked up a path to knock on a door.

It was a long moment before the door was opened by a woman with a narrow and even bony face, a black kerchief on her head. Her eyes had the exhausted and hollow look that comes from illness or lack of sleep and although she must have recognized Henry she did not show it.

"Mrs. Caporale, may I come in."

"If you want."

Her accent was heavier than Giancarlo's had been. As she led him through the narrow house he saw signs of children of various ages—hats and jackets, rag dolls, a slate board. She offered him the one armchair in the tiny parlour.

"You like something? Coffee maybe."

"No, thank you. I've just come to say how sorry I am about your husband."

She said nothing.

"He was a fine man."

Again nothing.

"He used to talk to me. Not like an employee but as a friend. He cared about other people more than most of us do."

She laughed, although what it meant he couldn't tell. "Yes, he cared. And now we are alone."

"What will you do?"

"Mr. Dawes give us some money. We go back to *Italia*. I take my children to my family."

Of course—money. He had been too concerned with his own grief. He took out his wallet.

"I hope this will help a little."

"Everything help." She took the money and put it in the pocket of her dress. "I remember now. Giancarlo left you something. It is here."

There was a small cabinet against the wall with a few books and a vase of silk flowers. She took an envelope from under the books and held it out to him. The envelope had been used before; he saw the Italian stamps on it.

"Some addresses. He write them down the same morning that is his last. Giancarlo think maybe you need them."

He rose from the chair to take the envelope and put it into an inner jacket pocket. "Thank you, Mrs. Caporale. I'm going to avenge your husband's death."

"Avenge it? This does me no good. It is Giancarlo I am angry at. He cared, yes, but what about us? What about me?"

She shook her head almost violently, but said nothing more.

Last winter he had built a mechanical chair for his father-in-law, with a system of clockwork-like adjusting wheels that Jeremiah Dawes had denounced as "too damn complicated." He had not seen the chair since, but now he found that Mr. Dawes had been wheeled on its vulcanized tires into the glasshouse. It was warm and close, but the old man had several blankets tucked neatly around him. He wore a pair of driving goggles, the lenses painted violet to keep out the light.

"What have you done to ruin my daughter?"

"I have no answer, sir."

"Of course, everyone will say that she is at fault. That she is a disgrace to my family and its good name. They will call her an adulteress. But I know differently. I know that it is because of you, not her. Your weaknesses. Your failures. And for the rest, that I can only guess at. But that you have driven her to this reckless behaviour I have no doubt. Naturally it follows that I, too, am to blame, for I supported you and welcomed you as a suitor. Do you know where they have gone?"

"Only that they did not wait for a train but took a pair of hired horses to Toronto."

"And what are your intentions?"

"I am going to find her."

"That is right. You will find her and bring her back, and we will make it known that she was taken against her will, or under some black spell or hypnotizing potion, by that degenerate Russian aristocrat. We will say that he had no time to sully her and that she is still your wife. We will restore her reputation. On the table beside me is a wallet containing a thousand dollars and a letter authorizing you to draw on my accounts. Any money you require you shall have. I will receive a telegraphic report from you every three days. I also have a list of men who will prove useful. They are powerfully connected—"

Henry said quietly, "No."

"What is that?"

"I know that she is your daughter and your last surviving child. But she is my wife. I do not want your money or your assistance. I shall find her on my own. What I shall do then I cannot say, but I have no intention of forcing her to return to me. My first, my only desire is to see her. After that I cannot say. I do not wish for your money or your list of men."

"Don't be an idiot, Henry. I pay your salary, I know how much you have managed to save. Take it."

"I have no intention of communicating with you in any manner. However, when I find her I will urge that she do so herself. I believe that Mr. MacMurtrie will do an excellent job as manager of the factory, quite possibly better than myself. Now I must leave if I am to catch the next train. Good day."

The old man's face was as rigid as stone. He raised a trembling hand and pushed the goggles from his eyes. "Look at me, Henry. I am a father without anything. Even the factory, my life's work, is going to fail. There is no hope for it. I cannot die this way. My daughter is all I have. Come here, come closer."

Henry did so. His father-in-law sat up and with his hand reached out to grasp the collar of Henry's jacket. "The women...our wives. We love them in the way we know. But we never understand..."

The words faded while his mouth continued to move soundlessly. Breath that smelled of dying. Henry gently pulled himself free and eased the man back in the chair. He walked through the house to the carriage, where he told James to move over, took the reins himself, and drove the horse down the road.

"Good God, Henry. Are you telling me you didn't know what was going on? You were living in the same house as this woman, eating at the same table, sleeping in the same bed. I may not know the first thing about matrimonial arrangements, but I find it quite fantastic."

It was the sort of dingy, beer-damp, roughhousing tavern he had always avoided. The air was fetid and the drunken stranger next to him kept leaning against his shoulder. The only advantage was that the other customers were too inebriated to eavesdrop. Just telling his friend the briefest account of events had exhausted his present capabilities. But he said, "I told you. I don't think anything did go on until I was here in Toronto."

"Yes, but I mean going on with Margaret. That she was, well, vulnerable to an advance."

"I knew that she was unhappy, but I did not understand why. There was always a touch of melancholy in her nature; I thought it might be increasing with time. Her brother's death made everything harder for her and the memory of her mother's death seemed to come back to torment her. Not long ago she even spoke of it while in a spell of delirium. Yet at other times I thought her unhappiness must be because of me, that I could not provide her with what she needed. The harder I tried the more I seemed to fail. It made me feel quite desperate. But I had not given up hope, not before this."

Chester sighed audibly, as if to show his sympathy. He pushed back his chair and drew a silver cigarette case from inside his jacket. Henry had hoped that his friend would have some answer, some direction for him; that hope had kept him from falling to pieces on the train. Chester absently played with the silver case.

"I suppose it doesn't matter what you knew or didn't know. The fact is that she's gone. The point—yes, the point is to show the world that you are still Henry Church. That your own position has not changed."

"I fear for her. He is a dangerous man, a political agent of some kind. A murderer."

"Henry, I am talking about you now, not her."

"I don't care about my position. I'm going to find Margaret."

"I do hope you are joking. Listen, Henry—" Chester leaned towards him and lowered his voice—"I know about love affairs and broken hearts. And when someone has left you for someone else there is nothing to do but get over it." He sat upright again. "Think of her this way. That she has jumped off a bridge. What is the point of jumping after her?"

"I need to speak to her. I need to ask if she really does not love me anymore."

"That is very touching. But I'm afraid she has already given you the answer. Henry, at this moment you have the public sympathy. You might not give two damns right now, but the truth is that we live within the confines of society, whether we like it or not. Even I must appear to live within these confines. You have done nothing yet to compromise yourself or lose your place. But if you go after her—well, people will think you are a fool. You will lose all respect. And really, Henry, what could be the good of it but to offer you more pain?"

Henry looked down at the table, ringed with countless stains. "I hadn't thought of that. Maybe that is what I want— to suffer more. Maybe it is the only thing I can feel. I don't know how to find her, Chester. How to uncover where she has gone. I thought that you might have some ideas."

"For you to save yourself, yes."

Henry stood up. "I asked you to meet me so that you could help me as I wish to be helped. If you will not, then I will find another way."

"All right. Sit down, Henry. There is no need to be melo-dramatic. If that is what you want, I can't stop you from making an ass of yourself. Let me think a minute. I need a cigarette. Where did I put those bloody matches?"

"Under your arm."

"Yes, right. I know. There's a fellow we use sometimes at the bank who investigates matters. Clients who turn out to have false identities, bad cheques, that sort of thing. His name is Alexander Brownwell. An odd sort, not someone you would want to invite to dinner, but with peculiar tal-ents. I believe he has an office down near the Gooderham and Worts distilleries. I can get the address in the morning.

I suppose your sort of unhappiness is just the kind of thing that puts bread on his table."

"I'll be at your office the moment it opens. Thank you, Chester."

"Don't thank me. I'm not doing you any good."

The distillery men on their way home carried with them the sweet odours of whisky and horse dung. They carried tin lunch pails and jostled one another in a joking manner; a younger fellow had his cap snatched away and thrown back and forth over his head, as if they were boys freed from school. How unimaginable, such lightness of spirit, but he could not even feel envy as he watched them turn off into one lane or another of small brick houses.

The address of Alexander Brownwell turned out to be several streets farther on, a modestly larger and much more decrepit house than its neighbours. The porch was half caved-in and littered with broken roofing tiles. Henry banged the door with the knocker, an incongruously grand lion's head.

A small square in the door above the lion slid open, an eye pressed to it.

"Who's there?"

"Henry Church. I sent you a note yesterday."

"Hang on a minute."

The square closed again and after a rattling of locks the door opened. Brownwell looked about fifty, with a moustache like a horse brush and a suit the colour of mustard. One of his large ears appeared to have a piece bitten out of it, a serrated scar just above the lobe. "Do come into the office, will you?"

Henry went in. Formerly the parlour, the office had as its only decoration a map of Toronto, dated 1878, pinned to the wall. "Please take a seat. Let me just get my notepad." The man picked it up from a rolltop desk, along with a stub of pencil, the end of which he licked as he sat down. "Yes, here it all is, already put down from your letter. Terrible troubles, Mr. Church. I have a wife myself, though where she is now I couldn't say, and you wouldn't see me paying anybody a nickel to find her. If you might just let me run through the particulars, to verify the facts of the matter."

Henry rubbed his knees. He did not care to look directly at the man and so kept his eyes on the map behind.

"Case of a runaway wife, name of Margaret Hope Church, daughter of the manufacturer Jeremiah Dawes. Victim of one Count Anatole Belinsky, citizen of Russia and a theatrical performer. Last known destination the Lakeview Hotel."

"That is all accurate."

"Do you have a likeness of her?"

"Is that necessary?"

"It immensely improves the chances of finding her. People who don't want to be found aren't in the general habit of giving out their real names."

"Of course. I do have this."

He reached into his jacket pocket and took out a photographic portrait taken the previous year. As Brownwell did not move, Henry had to rise from his chair to hand it to him.

Brownwell examined it closely without speaking, until Henry had to stop himself from snatching it back. "A handsome woman, indeed. Most understandable, the trouble one might receive from such as her. You'd be surprised though, the married women of no looks to speak of, who find men willing to engage in improper relations. This will be of immense help. A man seeing her, a ticket seller or porter, is likely to remember such a face. Unfortunately, there's been a considerable lapse of time, but the trail's not cold yet, as the Indians say. I'll find out where she's gone, Mr. Church. I require an initial fee of twenty dollars to cover my expenses."

Henry drew out his wallet. He could hear a long whistle from the distillery. Watching the wallet open, Brownwell ran his tongue along the edge of his bottom lip. These were Henry's acquaintances now, the world he had sunk to.

At the Bailey Hotel he did not have to fear meeting someone who knew him or Margaret. The toilet was down the hall, and each night the noise from the next-door tavern at closing woke him from his fitful doze. A day passed, a second. He took coffee in the room, paced at the end of the bed, lay down in his suit, and tried not to listen to the voices through the thin walls.

On the third afternoon he could no longer bear his room and descended to the small lobby to read the newspapers. Unable to make sense of the words, he went out and walked to the edges of the city. He passed foul tanners. Slaughterhouses with blood running down gutters and burly men in stained aprons hauling carcasses on their shoulders. He walked back again and stopped at his bank to learn the exact amount in his account. The savings from his own salary were modest, and his father-in-law had not yet ceded to the couple any of his fortune. The money would not last long.

Back in the room he paced again and then, as if touched by an electric shock, lunged for his trunk and reached to the bottom of it to find the leather-covered album of photographs. He sat in an armchair wedged in the corner and held the album in his lap, willing himself not to open it, not to torment himself, clutching it hard to prevent his fingers from moving. And although he could not have believed that there was an emotion he had not experienced in the last days, he felt again something different, a kind of intense yet frozen grief, as if he were already dead and should know this for eternity.

A hard rap on the door. Slowly he rose, put the album back in the trunk, and opened the door to see Alex Brownwell.

"Where is she? Where is my wife?"

"Let's not speak in the hallway, Mr. Church. I caution discretion for your own sake."

"Yes, yes, come in."

He closed the door behind Brownwell, who looked about the room and flared his nostrils, as if to record this hotel's particular dank smell. Henry said, "You must have found them. They are nearby."

"If I might have the rest of my fee, sir. Before divulging any information—that's standard practice. Another twenty dollars will clear up the bill."

"All right, all right. Here it is. Now go ahead."

"Absconded from the country, sir. The two of them together under his name. Count and Countess Belinsky."

"She has taken on his name?"

"Steady on, Mr. Church. Here, sit down a moment. Not legally, of course. It's perfectly common to use such a subterfuge in this situation, given the criminal nature of their relations. They might have been held up by the police. But now they have fled the jurisdiction, as we say."

"To where?"

"Europe is the best I can do. And Europe is a big place. They took a train to Montreal and boarded ship there. A nice voyage too, first class all the way to Le Havre. After that, it's anyone's guess. If I might offer some advice, perhaps the manly thing would be to let her go and seek an annulment in the courts. Seeing as you have no offspring, I'd say you've got a sporting chance. There's a member of the bar I know who is experienced in such cases."

Brownwell had placed his hand on Henry's shoulder, a professional offering of comfort that Henry shook off, standing up again. He would never seek an annulment. They *had* been married, had known love on their wedding night and other nights after. That could not be annulled. He said, "Perhaps they will return."

"Not much likelihood of that, if past experience is any judge. I'd say they're gone for good. I wrote down on this paper the name of the ship and the date she sailed, thinking that you'd want it. If you require my further services—"

"I think that will be all."

Brownwell adjusted his hat, which he had not removed, and touched the brim before leaving the room. Henry closed the door again and sank back into the chair. When he rose, his old life would be truly over. But what his new life was he could not see.

PART TWO

SPRING 1902

*T*he raven woke him. It hopped onto his bed, kneading the ratty blanket with its feet as it tried to find purchase, then stretched forwards to yank on his earlobe.

"Damn you, that hurts. All right, I'm getting up."

He swiped his hand and sent the bird squawking. As he sat up he pushed back his hair, which had grown down to his shoulders like that of some artistic madman, so that people sometimes stared at him in the street. He took some pleasure in that. The ropes strung under the mattress sagged as he got up and stumbled over to the corner to open the fly of his long johns and relieve himself in the tin pot by the washstand. At the basin he splashed cold water on his face and shaved with a long razor, trying to see himself in the mottled mirror hanging on the plaster wall. He had a weak chin—his old beard had hidden it.

The pearly light of morning softened the angles of the attic. He went to the table by the window and looked down into the Place Saint-André-des-Arts, where a peddler in a flat hat was pushing a cart of lampshades. The building across was a half-ruin, the balconies in near collapse, the painted advertisements on the exterior wall for Eau des Carmes Boyer and Chocolat Vinay peeling as if from leprosy. As he watched, a wagon rumbled into the square from the Rue Suger, pulled by a nag that ought to have been shot behind the ear out of kindness.

Emile must have emerged from the cellar below at the same moment, for he saw the hunchback start to cross the square with his peculiar gait. The bird skittered onto the window sill and called *crack-crack*, making Emile look over his shoulder.

"Henri, you're up? There's something I want to show you later."

"I can't be of much help."

"Can't or won't?"

"Watch out for the wagon, Emile. Before you get run down and we have to order an oversized box to bury you in."

"A coffin, not a box. Besides, don't you know that hunchbacks have nine lives, like cats?"

The wagon halted in front of the tavern, and Henry watched as Emile went round the back to help the driver unload casks of cider. Emile was a handsome fellow despite his deformity and always had some woman coming or going, and he seemingly unruffled by them. Henry pulled his head back in just as a tentative knock sounded on the door.

"Come in."

The door opened and the girl came in, carrying a tray on which balanced a bowl and a plate with a hard roll. She had her hair pulled back behind her freckled ears and wore a dress of indistinguishable colour, and she kept her eyes on the milky coffee so as not to spill it before placing the tray on the table.

"Thank you, Clothilde."

"Madame didn't want to send it up. I don't care who her husband was, she has the soul of a *bourgeoise*. She thinks that only people who can pay should eat—"

"It's good of you to defend me. But after all, Madame has some reason to be annoyed."

"Anyway, you better eat before that mangy bird of yours swallows everything in sight."

The raven had already skidded onto the table and now began to take vigorous pecks at the roll. Henry tore off a piece and threw it onto the window sill before dipping the remains in his coffee.

More formally, she said, "Madame wishes to know if you are going to pay something towards the rent by the end of the week."

"Tell her that is my full intention. If only the shop pays me."

"Madame is also wondering whether you are planning to get rid of the bird. She says that when you are away it terrorizes everyone else in the house. Her cats will not come out of their hiding places."

"Tell her I'm sorry but the bird must stay. That is the very reason I left my previous residence. And the one before that."

"I thought it was because you could not pay the rent there either."

"You are undermining my position."

He picked up the bowl with both hands and drank a quarter of it down. Then he glanced out the window again as Emile took a cask upon his back, shouting curses at the driver for letting it drop too hard. He could feel Clothilde's eyes on him but he resisted the impulse to look at her. She was twenty-two but she looked younger and was always about to burst out in either tears or complaints. And her thinness; she must have been starved in childhood.

"You should come to a meeting," she said.

"I don't care for meetings. And I'm not good with people."

"That's because people are impossible," she said huffily. She picked up the tray and left the room.

The address had been in the envelope given to him by Giancarlo Caporale's widow, but the place had no sign and he had had some difficulty in finding it all those months ago. On cautious inquiry he had discovered that everyone in the neighbourhood knew it as the bicycle repair shop run by the anarchists. Not much more than a shed, it was built against the remaining wall of an ancient chapel. It had a corrugated iron canopy jutting out over the sidewalk, beneath which Henry sat on a stool, repairing the spokes on the front wheel of a large delivery tricycle owned by the bakery in the Rue Descartes. The rider leaned against the wall smoking, his cap pulled low.

"I'll be just another ten minutes," Henry said.

"Makes no mind to me. Unless it starts to rain again. We've had nothing but rain this spring."

"What happened to these spokes? I've never seen any bent like this."

"You've never had someone run at you with a broom handle as a lance."

"A customer?"

"My twin brother. Apparently the failures of his life are my fault."

"But why is that?"

"Because I was born eight minutes earlier. I suppose everybody needs a reason."

He threw the end of the cigarette into the gutter. Henry detected a change in himself, a new interest in listening to other people explain themselves. He replaced and then tightened the last spoke, checking them all again for equal tension. From inside came the sound of hammering: Armand straightening a frame. Armand did not allow anyone to call him the owner, did not lock the cash box, was happy to accept goods in exchange instead of money.

The sound of the hammer ceased and a moment later Armand himself emerged from the shed, stuffing his gnarled pipe with tobacco.

"Your brother again?" he said to the rider. "He was one of us for a while."

"He was also a communist, a Blanquist, and a nihilist. He never sticks to anything for long. Thank you, Henri. The baker will send over a basket of fresh goods as payment."

The rider moved off on his tricycle, ringing the bell. Henry said, "I hope my landlady will accept brioches instead of rent money."

Armand drew on his pipe, dragging the flame into the bowl. He must have been at least sixty, although he still had a full head of curly hair. A large belly beneath the grease-stained apron. "Food and shelter," Armand said. "Basic human needs that ought not to be denied anyone. What the rich living in Passy spend on one meal could feed a family around here for a month. It is the economic structure that must change. But how can it until the human soul truly begins to express itself? That is the paradox that appears to defeat us. But if a small vanguard of truly free people can show the populace by example while exposing the current hypocrisy, perhaps then we will have a chance."

If anything, Armand had an even greater energy for speechifying than Giancarlo, and on a grander scale. Henry replied mildly, "Speaking of need, I think I'll walk over to Malvert's and buy an apple. I won't be ten minutes."

"That's all right, Henri. We don't punch a time clock here. I am not Mr. Henry T. Ford of the United States of America."

Malvert's fruit stall faced a triangle of grass formed by the convergence of the Rue de Babylone and the Rue de Sèvres. Henry sauntered over to buy his apple and stood a moment to watch a puppet show on the grass. The puppeteer had hauled his little stage on a cart, which was now pushed to one side. He stood inside the stage holding the two hand puppets above his head so that they appeared in the curtained space above. It was some French version of Punch, with the hook-nosed fellow giving Scaramouche some hard knocks with a bell—nothing original nor very artful, but it made the children laugh, except for one small boy who looked about to burst into tears. It was still appealing, this reduction of the human comedy to a miniature scale, our selves represented by cloth and papier-mâché with a bit of paint and glitter. It was safer somehow to depict the world this way, a parody of actual life, but at the same time it allowed certain emotions and thoughts, otherwise impermissible, to be expressed and even acted out. It made dark things acceptable and even alluring.

He'd never had such thoughts before, not when he was doing his own shows. Now Judy came up with the screaming baby, picked up the stick, and turned it on Punch. *Wack, wack, wack.* It was cruel and crude and tiresome really; Henry himself could do better. He walked back to the shop. As he arrived a boy came into the passage from the other side, pushing a bicycle that was too tall for him to ride. Armand came out. Despite his refusal of hierarchy, he preferred to greet each arriving customer and see what the work was about.

"Good morning, Monsieur Armand," the boy said. "The rear brake isn't working. My father asks will you accept a sack of onions as payment."

"We'd be delighted," Armand said. "Give them to your landlady, Henri. I'm sure she eats them raw, like apples."

At dusk the air grew heavy and almost opaque. He scrubbed the grease from his hands in the cracked sink in the shed, his nails remaining thin black moons. He shook hands with Armand and, taking the black bicycle that the man had given him, began his evening ritual. The bicycle had a battered frame and high handlebars with the rubber handgrips missing from the roughened ends, but the chain was new and the pedals turned well enough. He crossed the Seine and rode along the quais of the Right Bank, past the arcades and glittering shopfronts of the Rue de Rivoli. The women in their profusely decorated bonnets and their velvet-trimmed walking dresses, the men in their silk hats and double-breasted dress coats stared at his bizarre upright figure, not only on account of his long hair but also because of his height and the mismatched suit that hung on his limbs. But he stopped the bicycle only if he heard English or saw a woman of a certain shape and radiance of hair, sensed some possibility that it could be her.

The shops were already closing, the gates being noisily pulled down for the night. From them emerged more women and men, beribboned boxes piled in the arms of servants following behind. He had felt an indifference to such people in the past, if he had noticed them at all, if they had even existed back in his other life; now he wondered about them too, what sorrows they kept locked in their breasts.

He wheeled into the garden of the Palais-Royal, where, by the circular basin, an eight-piece military band was playing a march. Yet there was also a kind of fury that some-times welled in him, like an animal that had crept under his skin. Perhaps it was the thought of finding not her but the count, an eagerness to beat the life out of him. Along a side path of the garden came a boy using a flat stick to roll the hoop he ran beside. The small trees in neatly planted rows had new leaves. The sky had turned to pewter.

He felt a drop on his cheek. One of the tuba players blinked and looked up. Rain.

In a torrent.

The march collapsed and the musicians fled, trying to protect their instruments. The leader lost his round cap, which was trampled by the others. Henry stood as the garden became deserted and then he pushed his bicycle to a stone bench and sat down. Being drenched to the skin had the effect of slightly cooling the fire inside him. With a lit-tle luck he might even contract influenza and wheeze him-self to death, a coward's suicide.

At last he got up, his clothes so heavily soaked that they felt like sheets of lead draped over his shoulders. He went hulking through the rain on the bicycle. Even now, along the Rue des Petits Champs, he could not help trying to spot her under the bobbing domes of black umbrellas or through the streaked window of a cab. And it was all so fruitless since he did not even know where in Europe she might be now. He had exhausted his funds and grown tired of travelling, and it had seemed more likely that she would eventually come to Paris than anywhere else. It was a patheti-cally hopeful conclusion, it seemed to him now. He began to shiver. Even if she were here and not in England or Italy or even in Russia—even if they were here, it was foolish to think that he might find her this way when she could just as easily be hidden in that flower shop that was still open or behind that pedestalled bronze general or in a hotel twenty blocks away. The city was crowded with Parisians and Americans and British and Germans, choked with noise and dust, with nannies and horses and motor cars, with dogs, trams, omnibuses. No, not hopeful but mad. Well, let him be mad then, hatless, drenched, burning-eyed.

He passed a restaurant with a cast-iron stag over the transom and remembered that he had eaten nothing since that apple. The rain had fogged the edges of the front window, leaving a small oval through which he could see the profile of a woman sitting alone at a table. He knew almost before he saw her that she was Margaret.

Margaret.

He ripped open the door with both hands and threw himself into the restaurant, ignoring the waiter's shouts as he stumbled beseechingly towards the woman who was not Margaret, looked nothing like Margaret, who stared at him in terror.

He retreated again into the rain. And did not pause until he had ridden back to the Place Saint-André-des-Arts and his decrepit house. Leaning the bicycle against a courtyard wall, he climbed the staircase with the missing banister and, inside his room, dropped his clothes into a puddling heap. He brought down his fist upon his chest, swore and wept for his sick soul.

Poor as his own room was, he did not know how the hunchback could bear to live in the cellar of the house.

Descending the stone steps, Henry could smell the mould and rotting potatoes and coal dust. It was the one place the raven would not follow.

Emile had a bed of stuffed potato sacks and a broken chair upon which were slung a battered violin and small accordion, which he played on street corners when short of money. He had a long table made from stolen scaffold planks. "Not stolen," Emile had joked on Henry's first visit. "Appropriated for the cause." Madame's wine cellar was at the other end, the iron gate always locked and the enormous key among the jangling collection that dangled at her waist. Despite the chill, Emile was sitting at the table without a shirt. His deformed back looked as if an octagonal box had been slipped beneath the skin. He could not, Henry thought, have been much past twenty-five, but despite his easygoing spirit and his strength, he already had deep lines etched beneath his eyes that came from living in pain.

"Henri, here you are at last," Emile said over his shoulder.

"You did leave me a note, although I could barely make it out."

"If you had as little schooling as me you would write badly too. I am proof positive that you can't teach a boy to read and write by beating him. But never mind. Pour yourself a glass of wine. It's dull stuff, but all that Madame allows me for the work I do for her and maybe it will inspire you like last time."

On the table before Emile was the life-size figure of a man. In a military uniform, made from a blue suit with the addition of gold epaulettes and a row of tin medals. The plaster face had a chip out of the nose and one of the fingers had broken off as well.

"Have you solved your problem?" Henry said.

"No, it keeps confounding me. Serves me right for trying something above my station. I just don't have the brains for it. I can see part of the solution but not beyond, like there's a fog in my head. You see, we're going to put the general here up on top of the École Militaire. Have to do it at night of course, and there's a guard to get around, but in the morning it'll be visible right across the Champ de Mars. We'll do it next Tuesday night because in the morning the German and British high command are arriving and there'll be a big crowd gathered to watch those pompous asses get out of their motor cars."

"Well, what is it you are trying to say exactly?" Henry moved up to the table. He saw that the uniform was not specifically French, nor was the style of the painted beard.

"That we don't need the military anymore. That if there were no armies there would be no war. That the generals really are pompous asses."

"That seems simple. Why don't you just have the general's trousers drop, exposing his shorts? Or better yet have them go down and then up again, over and over. That will look ridiculous enough. I don't suppose it will cause a revolution, but it might make the crowd laugh."

"That's excellent. You do have a knack, Henri. But how to make it work? I haven't a clue."

"We'll need to lighten the trousers, cut away some of the material and replace the belt with a stiff wire attached to a rod. The rod will in turn be connected to the wheel of an electric motor."

"And what runs the motor?"

"A galvanic battery. The mechanism can go in a box

behind the general's heels. Do you think you can get what I need?"

"That's no problem. We'll appropriate it all for the cause."

"I don't know that it is worth the risk, Emile."

"Oh, but it is, Henri. The way it makes me feel—yes, it is."

On the stairway he encountered Clothilde, flying down with a basket of soiled linen piled up to her chin. He himself was carrying a crate under one arm. She did not see him until he called out her name, so that she started in fright and he had to grab hold of her and press her to the wall for fear of her tumbling over the edge to the tiles three floors below.

They stood catching their breath a moment. "You must be more careful," he said. "That's too fast. One day you're going to go over the side, Clothilde."

"I'm so used to it, Monsieur Cherche," she said, "that I think I could run up and down in my sleep. But I didn't see you. When I was a child my idiot brothers used to torment me by sneaking up to make me scream. I could hardly walk from the house to the barn without fear, and now whenever I come upon something suddenly it's as if I'm a girl again. I only hope they stay on the farm where they belong. You are back from the bicycle shop?"

"That isn't hard to guess, with all the grease on me. Some of the others, they stay almost clean all day long. But not me."

She tittered. "You have a spot on the side of your nose."

Involuntarily he raised one hand to rub at it, realizing an instant later that he had likely made it worse. "What have you got in there?" she said. "Not another bird, I hope. Or perhaps a monkey or a baby bear."

"Just some odds and ends of wood from the furniture shop on the Rue Serpente. I have an idea to make something. Did Madame let you change my bedding? I don't suppose so."

She lowered her voice. "I've taken it anyway."

"I don't wish you to get into trouble for my sake. Just now I've given the cook a horse shank, so perhaps Madame will feel lenient towards me for a while. But you have not finished your work. I won't keep you longer."

He pressed closer to the wall to let her pass, her arm lightly grazing his. "I will bring you fresh linen, monsieur," she said.

He walked up the rest of the way with some care and let himself into his room. Tossing the crate under the table, he stripped off his work clothes, scrubbed himself with cold water and rough soap at the basin, and dressed in his one dark suit with the frayed cuffs. The raven alighted on the sill of the open window and hiccuped at him. He took out a heel of bread and a handful of raisins from a tobacco tin and lay them on the desk. He brushed his long hair—an odd vanity, he reflected—and was about to depart when someone knocked on the door.

"Monsieur Cherche? It's me again—Clothilde."

He opened the door to see her holding two neatly starched and folded sheets. "Are you going out?" she said, not hiding her disappointment.

"I thought I would."

"To look for your wife."

"Who has told you that? Emile—"

"It wasn't his fault. I'm good at getting people to talk. Monsieur Cherche, I am through working in a few more minutes. Perhaps we could go to the brasserie down the street for a little supper. I have money, so that's no problem. And afterwards there is a meeting, not formal but just a few of our local people."

She had the palest blue eyes and freckles strewn across her oval face. Her orange hair was pulled back tightly. He watched her expression change from eagerness to something more needy.

"You will have a more pleasant evening without me, Clothilde. And there are so many young men who would only be too glad to share your company."

"Don't you see that anarchism could be an alternative to your mooning about? Monsieur Cherche, there is a larger world of real suffering and injustice out there, beyond our petty concerns. And, at the same time, we owe it to ourselves to live. I dislike men my own age, and Frenchmen in particular. Is it a crime to take some pleasure for oneself? But I see by your eyes that for you it really is some sort of crime. Oh, it is hopeless. Here—" She thrust the linen into his hands. "You can make your own bed."

She turned around and galloped down the staircase without pause. He considered calling her back but did not know what he could say and so merely put the sheets down on the mattress. He turned to go out and, seeing the crate on the table, stepped over to it and opened the lid. From it he picked up a small block of wood and a short piece of doweling. He held the block in the fingers of one hand, turned it slowly to the left, the right, made it nod. The dowelling he held just below and to the side like an arm. He raised it, turned it inward, made it bang against the block itself. Yes, he could draw something out of that wood. Not life, as Clothilde put it, but pretend-life, mock-life. He let the pieces clatter back into the crate and quickly went out the door.

That evening he searched for her in the neighbourhood of the Parc de Monceau, from the Boulevard Haussmann to the Place Malesherbes. After all, even a madman should conduct his affairs in an orderly fashion. He felt the prick of a cobbler's nail come up through the sole of his right boot as he pedalled, an almost pleasant irritation. Tonight he saw neither her nor any woman who could fool him for even a moment and send his heart racing. He rode until darkness fell and the street lamps came on along the main boulevards, the side streets dark but for the light spilling from the taverns and cafés. Until it was past midnight, and then he kept riding, struggling up Montmartre and through the gates of the dark cemetery. He wheeled on the neatly maintained paths, passing the family vaults and bronze figures on pedestals. He stopped at a marble statue of a girl—no, an angel, for she had the most exquisite wings folded behind, her arms thrown over a tomb and her head laid down in grief. He reached out to touch her cold face.

Out of the cemetery and into the narrow streets from which could be seen the still unfinished Sacré Coeur. Church of the Sacred Heart and, over it, the moon. Dank smell of cellars and badly cooked food and spilled wine.

Figures in the shadows of doorways, voices and laughter. A woman called to him, "Monsieur Cherche, why not try something different tonight? Someone with some real flesh on her bones." Yes, they knew him by name and even by his taste. The woman calling to him from under a gaslight had a doughy face and enormous breasts, each the size of a man's head, which she showed by hiking up her entire dress. "You will find some comfort in these, I promise you." He managed to tip his hat and mutter, "Thank you, no, mademoiselle."

Three more whores called to him, but he had been with all of them before and he never went to the same one twice. In the doorway of a *brocanteur* whose window was crowded with old junk stood a woman with a good figure, though her face was gaunt and made more narrow by the yellowish hair hanging down. Her eyes looked at him only for a moment and then down again. Her lips looked puffy, as if someone had struck her. She was perhaps forty.

"Good evening," he said. "I have not seen you before."

"I'm from Lyon. Things were slow there. You wish to come upstairs?"

"If you do not mind."

"You can pay?" She looked at him doubtfully; the earlier shyness had been an act.

"Yes, of course."

The stairway was unlit and smelled of tar. She opened a door at the first landing and led him into a room lit only by the moonlight. Pasted to the walls were pictures from the illustrated newspapers of society women in carriages or strolling in gardens. A pile of clothing had been thrown onto the only chair. The bed was pushed into the corner. An enamel bowl and pitcher of water stood on a small table. She stepped towards him and, taking his hand in her own, placed it on her breast. With her other hand she reached into his trousers.

"Still curled up there? Don't worry, I won't bite. Wake up, sleepyhead."

She crouched, undid the buttons of his trousers, and began to lick the base of his scrotum. He saw how her hair grew from a point outwards, in a perfect spiral, one of nature's forms. He said, "May I ask a favour?"

"Of course, monsieur. If you wouldn't mind paying first."

"Forgive me." He fumbled for his money. She put the bills on top of the clothing on the chair and then stepped out of her dress and removed her underthings. He said, "Would you be so kind as to wet your hair at the bowl? Perhaps your breasts as well."

"But the water is cold. Ah well, as you wish."

He stood watching her as she bowed her head over the bowl and poured from the pitcher. She let it drip onto her shoulders, arms, and breasts. He took off his own clothes—he was hard now—and led her to the bed, gently lay her down. As he came, he caressed her damp hair with his hands and whispered, "Margaret, Margaret."

After a few moments she shifted from beneath him and, standing again, used a threadbare towel to dry her hair and privates. "You can find me here most nights, monsieur. And you are welcome to call me anything you like."

"Yes, yes, thank you," he said, pulling on his clothes too quickly and getting his foot caught in the trouser leg.

"So who is this Margaret anyway?"

"My wife."

She sighed. "A man who goes to a whore and thinks of

his wife—that is having things the wrong way round, monsieur."

"Monsieur Cherche, I insist you open up!"

"What's that?" He roused himself painfully from sleep. He had no idea of the time or even the day of the week. "Madame? But I am not dressed."

"This has gone too far." She continued to rattle the door, as if she would pull it off its hinges. "Do you think this is the charity ward? If you can't pay you have to get out. Do you understand? I'll have your few things thrown out the window and into the street. I'm fed up with you and that lice-infested bird of yours."

"All right, madame. I hear. Give me one more month, that's all I ask. I'll pay everything I owe. If you throw me out now you won't get any of it. Allow me to pay my debt to you."

"One month? I shouldn't give you one more day. I am too soft-hearted and you are taking advantage of me, Monsieur Cherche. If Armand were not a friend of mine, I wouldn't even consider it. All right, one month and not a minute longer. If you do not pay, out you go."

"Thank you, madame."

He heard her make a sound through her nose and clomp heavily away in her clogs. He pushed off the blanket and stretched. Splashed cold water on his face. Dressed, he went over to the table and stared out the window. It must have been Sunday, for the square was deserted and he could hear church bells. From under the table he pulled out the crate and, searching through the cast of pieces of wood, he found a rectangle of pine about the size of his hand. He put it in the table clamp borrowed from Emile, a clumsy iron thing that slipped twice before he got it adjusted right. The carving tools he had bought from a carpenter's shop near the river. He picked a chisel and, holding it against the corner of the block, lightly tapped the wooden handle with a mallet. A little pyramid of wood fell to the floor. He worked on, rounding the block while the raven watched suspiciously from the window, half raising its wings and settling them again.

He would need just three marionettes. The Wife. The Husband. The Count. No, not the Count but the Prince, as in a fairy tale. The Wife he would give large almond eyes, a fine pointed nose, full lips. The Husband: large ears, surprised eyes, a mouth bent in a painful smile. And the Prince would be squat, bowlegged, all exaggerated bulges and an open, hungry mouth. Fourteen parts for each body—torso and pelvis, upper and lower arms and legs, hands, feet. Leather strips for easy and natural movement, the joints shaved thin. For the Wife and the Prince he would need fully carved bodies—a burly chest with black curls of lambs' wool for him, breasts sanded to silkiness for her. There would be no more roaming nights, as he had too much work to do.

A knock on the door. "Who is it?"

"Clothilde. I've got your breakfast."

"It's not locked."

He did not look up as she put the tray down on the far end of the table. "What are you making?"

"A puppet. With strings. To pay the rent."

"Henri," she said. It was the first time she had ever used his first name. "Every day I salt your food with my tears."

She turned to leave and still he did not look up but waited for the sound of the closing door. He spoke aloud in a voice higher and breathier than his own. *Read me a poem, will you, dear? No, not Keats, it makes me sad. You must take care of me, you must protect me from the world.* Another stroke of the chisel. He tried another voice, deeper, with a guttural accent. *My father wished to drown me, that's how unwanted I was. But it only made me stronger. When I grew up I took my vengeance. And now when I want something I take it.* Two light, deft strokes, angling out the chin. In a voice almost his own but with a slight tremor. *I am not worthy of you.*

He put down the chisel and picked up a knife. The eyes had to be most expressive, had to give the puppet the illusion of a soul. Except for the Prince, of course; the Prince's eyes would be small, dark, shallow. Soulless.

"Henri, do you really think anyone will come to your puppet show? Forgive me, but it doesn't seem likely."

"We'll just have to see."

He was fitting a leather joint between the carved upper and lower right leg of the Husband. Taking the leather out again, he laid it on the table to pare it thinner.

"Do you know the number of theatres in Paris?" said Emile, lying back on Henry's bed with his hands behind his head. "There's the Opéra Comique, the Gymnase, the Vaudeville, the Variétés, the Lyrique—I can't remember them all. You can see equestrian performances at the Nouveau Cirque and the Palace, acrobats at the Médrano. And those are just some of the big ones. What about all the cabarets and the small theatres—too many to count, Henri."

Henry shrugged. He fitted in the leather piece again. Yes, it bent more naturally. Now he would use carpenter's glue and small tacks to hold it. All day the voices of his characters spoke inside his head so that when someone at the bicycle repair shop addressed him he did not hear and had to be shouted at or tapped on the shoulder. At night he lay in bed and sketched out the wooden controls, which by necessity had to be more complicated than he had used in the past. He wanted the most natural movement, graceful sometimes and brutal at others.

"Henri? Did you hear me?"

"I'm sorry."

Emile scratched behind his ear. "I think your mattress has bedbugs. I don't know, Henri. I admit you look less miserable lately. But not less crazy."

"I don't know how to take that."

"And tell me, what are you going to do for music? Surely even a puppet show needs an instrument or two for atmosphere."

"It's true. I was thinking of your accordion and violin, Emile."

"Really?" He sat up. "I've never performed for an audience that wasn't trying to push me off the sidewalk."

"Of course I'll pay you something."

Emile got onto his feet. "Let me get them now. We can start working it out."

"No, I'm not ready."

"Then maybe I just ought to go and practise. I'm a little rusty."

"A very good idea."

"We'll have a drink later, Henri." The door closed

behind him. Henry smiled to himself. He picked up another strip of leather and began to pare it. It was for her that he was doing this. A gift for her, even if she couldn't know it. The Husband figure was done, unpainted and unclothed and unstrung, but finished. He held it up by the head and shoulders so that the feet just touched his knee. "Sit down, Henry," he said aloud and the puppet came down, crossing its legs and putting a hand to its chin. "Enjoy the quiet while you can. Because I'm afraid I'm going to have to make you suffer." The Husband tilted his blank face up at him as if in inquiry.

A knock on the door. It seemed that he had become more popular now that he hardly left his room.

"Henri, put down those puppets for a moment."

"Wait a moment, Clothilde." With his most delicate knife he was carving the fingers of the Wife, the right hand slightly cupped.

"There." He looked up and saw her in the doorway, wearing her coat and hat. At the other end of the table the raven was rearranging the extra scraps of leather. "I want to ask a favour of you," he said.

"What is it?"

"If you would help me with the costumes. I know how I want them to look, I've even bought the material. But I'm not much of a seamstress."

"I ought to say no."

"I'll pay you. Or do some of your chores. I know how overworked you are already."

"Don't insult me. I was coming to ask you to attend a

meeting with Armand, Emile, and me. The cart is waiting for us in the courtyard."

"Clothilde—"

"If you come I'll do the sewing for you."

"It doesn't seem fair to you somehow."

"I've long ceased expecting things to be fair. Are you coming? We can't wait forever."

"One moment," he said, getting up. "Let me get my coat."

"And you better use the water closet downstairs. The trip isn't a short one."

The man driving the cart had a persistent cough. The five of them—they had picked up a fellow along the way—huddled in the back, saying little after the first mile. When they reached the outskirts of Paris, Henry ceased to recognize any landmarks and the wheels of the cart jarred against the rutted dirt road. The horse finally halted before an inn. They got down and stretched and went into the back room, where seven other people were already assembled, two women among them, one with an infant at her breast. They sat on chairs brought in from the restaurant and drank poor wine while an elaborate process was begun that resulted in the choice of a young farmer, twisting a shapeless hat in his hands, to conduct the meeting without holding any actual authority over the others.

Armand said, "I wish to introduce our friend Henri Cherche. He is from distant Canada and a friend of our late *camarade*, Giancarlo Caporale."

"Henri is a former member of the ruling class brought down by circumstance and conscience," added Emile.

The situations in Russia and Spain were reported on, followed by a discussion of a recently published pamphlet in Toulouse. "It's a regurgitation of Déjacque," declared the oldest man present, who appeared to Henry to be in his seventies. "Criminality and violence will only set us back. We must write a pamphlet in response." Henry felt his eyes begin to close. He had been working late every night. He opened them suddenly when Emile nudged his foot and the young farmer asked if there was any more business.

"Yes," Clothilde said. "I wish to open a discussion on the deplorable conditions of women in this country. They have few property rights—"

"Property is an evil," said the woman with the infant.

"Of course it is an evil. But while it exists, women must not be inferior to men. As I say, they have few property rights, they are deprived of any social position if they refuse to marry, and yet they are condemned by both church and state for sexual involvements outside of marriage."

"But you have always refused me, Clothilde," said the young farmer.

"That's my right, too, Fréderic, so don't make an ass of yourself. And what of the oppressive institution of marriage itself? Our visitor, Henri Cherche, is a perfect example."

Armand said, "What are you going on about, Clothilde?"

"We are supposed to welcome this Henri among us. But all he does is moan over his wife for running off with another man. Can you think of anything more bourgeois? More self-centred? Was she his chattel? Marriage only leads to jealousy and possessiveness. A man and a woman are not one body and spirit but separate beings. Only when that separateness is recognized can they meet in equality. Love can dwell only in an atmosphere of freedom. But this Henri cannot rise above his petty emotional needs. He is the worst kind of fraud."

Her voice had grown to a near shriek, her blush rising from her thin neck to her forehead as she sat down again. Henry stood up. "I don't mean to fool anyone. My friends here have been kind and generous to me, far beyond what I deserve. To have offended such a person as yourself, Clothilde, is unforgivable. All I can do is apologize."

He felt the silence weigh heavily on them all. Armand got up and put his hand on Clothilde's shoulder.

"I am sorry," Clothilde said through her hands. "I don't know what came over me."

"That's all right," Armand said. "Anarchists, too, have a right to their unhappiness."

At that everyone rose from their chairs, shook hands, and departed.

He had not yet found a theatre in which to perform, but in the meantime he blocked out a space in the attic room, hung the puppets up behind him on an oak coat rack, and worked out the play. In the blocked-out space was set a miniature parlour: chairs, a tiny plush divan, even a little fireplace with a flickering light—a hidden candle—inside. At this moment the Wife was sitting on the divan, her skirts spread before her, and the Husband, wavering a moment on the points of his feet, went down onto his knees and then placed his head upon her lap. The Wife's hand descended gently upon the back of his head.

The strings became tangled, the Wife's hand string with the two head strings of the Husband. He shook the Wife's control, which only made it worse. "Damn," he said aloud. Holding both controls in one hand, he leaned down to separate them. How long had he been at it? At least three hours. His head ached and there was a deep soreness in his chest. He hung up the marionettes.

"Come on," he said to the raven. Perched on the footboard of the bed, it had been preening under one wing. "Let's get some air."

He thought that he might see Clothilde on the way out, but she was nowhere about. She had been avoiding him these last days. In the courtyard he picked up his bicycle and mounting it, he wobbled a moment before gaining speed. Up the street to Place St. Michel, crowded at the end of the day, and across the bridge to the island. Every so often he caught a glimpse of the raven, nipping a crust of bread from under a café table or rousting some pigeons from the shoulders of a statue. He wheeled in front of the cathedral and saw the little groups of travellers, the ladies holding their parasols and reading their red-covered Baedekers, the men taking a cigarette before going inside. He could not imagine what it felt like to be one of them.

On the other side of the island he rode along the quai. At the Pont au Change he dismounted and walked the bicycle onto the bridge, stopping halfway. While trams and pedestrians crossed behind him, he leaned on the stone rail and looked down at the Seine. The raven landed beside him, pulled at his coat collar, and then dove towards the water before rising again and disappearing somewhere. The river was more grey than usual, and as he watched it flow steadily beneath the bridge he felt the soreness of his heart. Beneath the water he saw a dark form move towards the bridge and hover there. Perhaps it was the shadow of a cloud or more likely some sunken debris. It circled beneath the water, became motionless again, and then drifted under the bridge.

He turned the bicycle around. He would go back to the attic and work into the night.

Above the door, in letters formed by glass shards pressed into the mortar, were the words "Théâtre Sous le Pont." Henry kicked the door with the heel of his shoe, waited, kicked again.

A muffled voice from inside and then the door opened upon a corpulent man, triple-chinned. "Come in, come in," the man said, his voice garbled as if from stones tucked in his cheeks. "I'm René Comeau. I think you'll like the little space I've got here. All right, it's not exactly the Théâtre Sarah Bernhardt, but for the right show, an intimate piece, avant-garde even, it's a shoe that fits just so. You'd be surprised to find who likes to crawl out of the woodwork to see a little performance at the Sous le Pont. Just watch your head, Monsieur Cherche, that first beam's a little low. As you can see, there's no need for a ticket booth, you just put a boy on a stool and you're in business. No, no, don't go through yet. Before I push aside this little curtain—that tear is easy to fix—you need to imagine a body in every seat in the house."

That wasn't hard; there were only fifty or sixty seats, in seven battered rows that looked to have been salvaged from some larger, condemned theatre. The space sloped precariously down to the stage, which was raised no more than three feet and contained by a low arched ceiling. Gaslights with tin reflectors, a patched velvet curtain drooping from a rope.

Henry walked down the aisle and sat in the second row. His knees jammed up against the seat in front.

"The theatre's been dark for two months now. A real shame, artistic potential like this going to waste." Monsieur Comeau was eating sunflower seeds, taking them from one wide trouser pocket and placing the empty shells in another. He came down the aisle too, but continued to the stage and hauled himself up with a groan. "The last fellow who performed here dreamed of playing the cabarets. In regular life he was a postman. He was a big man but unfortunately he had a soprano voice. Sweated something awful. On the first night the audience laughed so hard that the poor fellow jumped down from the stage, ran to the bridge, and threw himself into the Seine. Fortunately, his costume billowed with air and he floated for a good half mile or so. One of the barges fished him out with a gaff. Before that there was a husband and wife, mime artists or so they called themselves, and she a good twenty years older than he. *La Symphonie de mécanique,* it was called, very modern and tedious beyond compare. Yes, an endless stream of hopefuls and stage-struck types, Monsieur Cherche, going back to the First Republic and before. Why don't you come up and see how it feels."

Henry had been examining the seats on either side, the horsehair stuffing flattened hard or leaking from the seams. Monsieur Comeau came off the stage and Henry leapt up. There was just about enough room. Nor did he need more seats in the audience; it was likely he couldn't fill them, not with what he had planned.

"How much for a month?"

"Well, I can't let it go for nothing, you know. There's the upkeep for one thing. And the historic significance for another. Just this morning I had another inquiry, from a woman who does an impersonation of several female murderers on the witness stand. Very compelling. I couldn't take less than a thousand francs."

"I'll give you six hundred."

"Monsieur must be intending to perform a comic act. I will accept eight hundred, but you have to clean the place up yourself."

"Agreed, if you will let me pay four hundred now and the rest at the end of the first month."

"At least tell me what sort of show I am taking this chance on."

"Puppetry."

Monsieur Comeau looked as if he had bit into a rancid seed. "For children?"

"Adults."

"In French?"

"English. My French isn't good enough."

"You are lucky that I am sympathetic to artistic need. Many years ago I wrote a show for the music hall with a friend. He flattered me and asked me to put up the money, which he then ran away with before we even opened. Still, sometimes I think of trying again. If you don't mind, monsieur, I would at least like the four hundred francs now."

Henry took them from his pocket, the last of his savings. He had nothing now. Monsieur Comeau folded the bills and slipped them into the same pocket as the empty shells. "Here is your theatre then," he said, gesturing to the stage. "I shall come myself to see your opening night, even if I do not speak your language, which as far as I can tell is unsuitable for artistic endeavours. I only hope that I shall not find myself alone."

Henry hoped so too. He wanted an audience, people he did not know. He jumped from the stage and walked quickly up the aisle, slapping the seats as he passed.

Au Théâtre Sous le Pont, VI
commencer le 1er Mai, à 22 heures
THE STOLEN WIFE
Un tragedie avec des marionettes présentée par M. H. Church
Billets 3 francs chacun

The Wife put her hand to her forehead and half turned away. A long, lugubrious note on the violin.

"But why do you have to go? You know I don't like it when you are away."

"No more than I do. But it can't be helped. Your father commands me."

"You should stand up to my father."

"But, my sweet, I owe him so much."

"You are afraid of him, I think."

"Don't say that. Now, you promised me that you will let the Prince paint your portrait while I am gone."

"But I am not comfortable in his presence."

185

The Wife turned around again. The Husband reached out, touched her hand.

"I know. His ways are brusque. But to have a portrait of you would mean so much to me. I can stand before it and worship you."

"A woman doesn't want to be worshipped. She wants..."

"What, my darling? Tell me."

"It is no matter. But I don't like the way the Prince looks at me."

"Come to me, my wife."

A long, passionate kiss accompanied by a melodious line of the violin.

"Ah, my husband. No one but you can kiss me with such tenderness. Let us go... upstairs."

"There isn't time. I must catch my train. Until I am back, my love! Think of me!"

The Wife's arms reached out, but the Husband receded, his feet sliding backwards as if pulled by some magnetic force. Alone, the Wife stood with her hands at her sides and her head down. The violin melody quickened, descended into the lowest notes. A sharp rap and the music abruptly stopped.

The Wife's head came up.

"Who is that?"

The Prince entered, bouncing on his short legs. Even so, he looked enormous in comparison to her, in uniform of scarlet and gold braid, bald head polished and shining. He stopped halfway to her. Slowly the Wife turned.

On the first night, an audience of twelve, including the landlord Comeau, Armand, and several mechanics from

186

the repair shop. Alone in the front row sat Clothilde. Even as he performed, he could hear the young woman weeping. As for the handful of others, as Emile said before the curtain went up, "The devil knows what brought them here."

Emile sold the tickets. And turned down the oil lamps along the walls. And pulled the curtain open before taking his place in a corner below the stage with his instruments. Henry stood on the stage, unhidden by screen or sheet, an undertaker in a black suit, a giant standing inside a house. In each hand he held a complicated wooden control. His awareness of the handful of people in the seats did not vanish but rather merged with his consciousness as he performed, as if they were a part of the performance. Even the sound of Clothilde's weeping was a part of it.

"Oh God, leave me alone, I say!"

"You are a goddess needing defilement. Your beauty is wasted on a mere husband, the lowest form of creation. I shall take you by force, if necessary! Ah, what a delicious feast beneath those clothes!"

"Husband, save me!"

"Your husband is weak and stupid. Besides, he is far away, where husbands belong. And he will be farther still when I take you away with me."

"Surely you will burn in hell for this sin."

"We will both burn. And what does it matter? We are all kindling anyway."

On the second night, twenty-one tickets sold.

On the next, forty.

On the fourth, carriages pulling up at the passage entrance and men descending in dress coats, silk hats, kid gloves. Women with fans and half-masks before their faces, hiking up their skirts and wrinkling their noses as they entered.

On the fifth night, half as many turned away. A dozen argued with Emile at the entrance until he allowed them to stand at the rear. Many could not speak English.

Backstage, Emile said, "You are a *succès de scandale,* Henri. Everyone wants to see the show before the police shut you down."

The landlord Comeau said, "I cannot believe it. I am astounded. Speechless. Never have I seen a phenomenon like it. Society people paying money to see wooden puppets fornicating on a stage. You are a true artist, Monsieur Cherche, a perverse genius."

"That is not the genius," Emile said. "To me it is the moment when the Wife realizes that she is falling in love with her captor. What that must cost you to perform each night, Henri—"

"Of course the rent I am charging you is ridiculously low," Comeau interrupted. "I've been far too generous a benefactor. The next month it must go up another three hundred francs."

"We'll find a bigger theatre," said Emile. "Four times as many seats."

"No," Henry said, brushing down his coat. "We'll remain here. Perhaps they come for the wrong reasons. Does it matter? Well, come on, Emile. It is time for us to begin again."

Despite his exhaustion each night, he could not sleep. During the day he rode the black bicycle, not to look for her anymore but out of an unappeasable restlessness. He cycled to the edge of the city and beyond: Vincennes, Meudon, St. Cloud. Watching the houseboats on the Seine or farmers moving their cows into pasture.

Always he was back in time for the show at the Sous le Pont. He had believed it to be a gift for Margaret, but now he thought it was for him, for what he needed just to survive. And yet it felt as if the performances were slowly killing him, like a little more arsenic in his food every day, the poison gradually destroying him from the inside.

On the last performance of the third week he decided not to take his bows, and never to take them again. Instead, he left the stage immediately, slipping on a worn suede coat that he had found in the theatre one night, and wheeled his bicycle out the back door. He rode it through the dark streets, tires bouncing on the stones, back to the Place Saint-André-des-Arts. Leaving it in the courtyard, he climbed the stairs in the dark, feeling along the upstairs passage for his door. Inside, he lit the lamp on the table.

A sound. He turned to see Clothilde stirring awake on his bed. She had in one hand the string of black pearls and beside her lay the photograph album.

"Henri? You're back."

"What are you doing, Clothilde?"

She sat up. "I brought you a brandy. I thought it would help you to sleep. It's there on the table."

He took the pearls from her hand and put them back in the box. He looked over at the album but left it on the bed. Clothilde saw his eyes upon it but said, "That ugly bird of yours came in through the window but when he saw it was just me he flew out again."

Henry picked up the glass of brandy and took a sip. "This is Madame's good brandy. I wouldn't want her to find out."

"These days she's too busy hiking up her skirts for that face-powder salesman who lives on the second floor to notice a thing. How was the show this evening?"

"I prefer not to speak of it."

"Well, I think it's a terrible thing, offering yourself up like that each night. It's humiliating and worse. It's time to feel something else, something good for a change."

She came towards him, her hair in disarray and her washed-out dress creased from lying down. She placed her hands on the sides of his face. Her palms were hot against his skin. He looked into her pale eyes and saw the neediness of her mouth and he felt himself wanting her but he took her hands gently away from his face. She did not step away but continued to look at him, though her eyes changed.

"Don't worry, I'll leave you alone. Emile wanted to take me for a drink anyway."

"Clothilde—"

"Why do you have those photographs, Henri? To punish yourself? Or perhaps that is your idea of pleasure. I considered taking them to the kitchen and throwing them into the fire but then I realized that it is not my work. I can't do it for you. Well, goodnight, Henri."

He heard her go down the stairs and went to the window. After a time she came out with Emile and the two of them crossed the courtyard to the bar on the other side. They walked close together but not touching, Emile talking with animation while Clothilde had her shoulders hunched up defensively, as if she knew that he was watching. When they were gone he lay down on his bed. He thought it might still be warm from her having lain there, but the sheets were cold. From the window he heard laughter. Time passed. The oil lamp dimmed but did not go out. He moved his hand and touched the edge of the photograph album. He moved his hand away. But his hand moved back of its own accord. Touched the cover. Began pulling it towards him.

Just inside the narrow archway that led to the bicycle shop stood a spindly tree. The ragmen who used the next courtyard to sort their rags had to pull their carts around the tree and for the last months he had wondered why they did not simply cut it down. But today he saw why: white blossoms almost dizzying in their lushness, and the air heady with scent.

He had forgotten to eat again and as he bicycled away the perfume lingered in his nostrils and made his stomach turn over. He had no particular destination in mind but as he came to the Luxembourg Gardens he decided to rest a moment so that the pain might ease. He walked his bicycle past the palace to the stone-lipped, octagonal pond, where an old woman in a Normandy cap rented toy sailboats. He watched three boys sailing their boats, directing them with long bamboo sticks. A lost memory came to him, of having once built a little boat of his own out of a patent-medicine box and a tin paddle-wheel powered by a bit of wound-up India rubber. He had let it putter across a large puddle that remained in the field after the spring rain, until one of the masters had confiscated it. *With cause*, the master had said, but what had it been? He had spent nights trying to figure out what he had done, but never could he discover an answer.

An attendant came by and Henry paid him a few centîmes for a metal chair. He turned the chair towards the sun and stretched out his legs. Closed his eyes. A rattle made him open them again and he saw that an American in a bowler hat had taken the chair next to him and was rattling his *Herald Tribune*. Henry closed his eyes again. How tired he was and how everything seemed to ache. His head, his jaw, his ribs, each breath he took...

He stirred himself awake. His shoulders were stiff and his neck cramped from his head having fallen back. The sun was lower in the sky. The three boys were gone and instead five carriages were lined up along the gravel path, their nannies sitting on the benches behind and talking. A man pushed a praline cart along the path, the smell of burning sugar wafting from it. Henry sat up straighter and stretched out his arms. On the chair next to him was the *Herald Tribune* left by the American. He hadn't read a newspaper in weeks and he picked it up to idly turn the pages.

UNUSUAL PERFORMANCE AT THE LYRIQUE

Myth Comes to Life
In Watery Spectacle

Special to the Herald Tribune, Paris Edition

Theatre-goers who have attended any of Count Anatole Belinsky's previous performances in this city know why he is billed as the Strongest Living Man and the Human Whale. With a combination of rough charm and brute animal force he wins over his audience, performing conventional feats of strength. But it is in the third act of his new entertainment, entitled "The Mermaid of Paris" and now showing on the Blvd. St. Martin, that Count Belinsky adds a new and daring twist to his program.

The curtain rises to a pleasing scene in which the Russian, dressed in the striped linen jacket and straw hat of the Sunday holiday-goer, is rowing a small boat, the water beneath simulated by the waving of a long blue silk. Sitting in the front of the boat is an attractive woman, who, curiously, is not named in the printed program. The woman holds a parasol over her head and acts in a demure yet flirtatious manner. This appealing courtship is performed in pantomime, accompanied by a light musical score. In a dramatic gesture, the count gets down on one knee to propose to the lady, but he loses his balance and plunges over the side, disappearing behind the boat. Naturally the lady becomes distraught, putting her hand to her forehead. She faints and falls back into the boat.

At this point the boat and the blue silk are drawn off the stage and after a musical crescendo the second curtain opens to reveal a large, six-sided glass tank, upon which coloured lights are playing and making the water shimmer. From somewhere above, a body plunges into the tank; it is Count Belinsky himself, and the audience realizes with a gasp that they are witnessing his "fall" from the boat. Struggling out of his clothes, the count reveals a bathing costume beneath. But his energy and air expended, he sinks senseless to the bottom of the tank and lies there for what seems an eternity until the audience begins to call out for the management to take action.

It is just then that a large clamshell in the bottom corner of the tank opens. From it emerges a mermaid of striking beauty, her upper torso clothed in only the most diaphanous silk, which hides almost nothing. This mermaid, played by the woman from the boat scene, is a true miracle of theatrical illusion, for it is impossible to understand how the glittering scales of her lower half, which narrows and then widens again into a fin, could be so convincingly constructed. Even more remarkable is the movement of this maid of the sea as she turns, arcs, and even somersaults with a most entrancing grace. Indeed, the woman's talent is so great that one might be tempted to speculate that she is a fellow national of the count and a former member of the famous Ballets Russes.

One touch from this divine creature's hand is enough to revive him. Just how Count Belinsky manages to stay submerged for so long has been subject for much conjecture. The most convincing theory is that a source of air is hidden inside the clamshell, to which the count periodically swims or drifts and so renews himself. The same possibility cannot be considered for the mermaid, who never once returns to the shell. What follows is an underwater dance between man and maid of a very suggestive and risqué nature.

This dance reaches its climax just as a more frightening sea creature emerges from the clamshell. This octopus, a most cleverly worked contraption, was seen in the count's previous show. This time the octopus knocks the count insensate to the floor of the tank (his head conveniently falling at the edge of the clamshell) and proceeds to attempt a ravishment of the mermaid. The sight of a beautiful and nearly naked sea nymph being tossed about keeps everyone watching breathlessly.

Just as the octopus subdues our lovely mermaid and her head falls back helplessly in a swoon, the lights go out. The orchestra plays tempestuously until the lights come up again and once more the little boat floats upon the lake. The pretty lady is just recovering from her faint and the audience realizes with a smile that the preceding underwater drama was meant to be a dream. Now the count emerges from behind the boat, dripping wet and laughing. The woman embraces him in relief and the count, looking over her shoulder at the audience, offers a large and knowing wink.

Whether this performance is art or something else we leave for the reader to decide should he choose to attend. We can, however, confidently promise an evening of high sensation. The show is presented six nights a week for an indefinite run. Tickets range from ten francs for the rez-de-chaussée to two for the second balcony, and are already selling briskly.

Calmly, calmly he folded the newspaper, tucked it under his arm, and rose from the chair. On his first step his leg nearly gave out under him, but he recovered and picked up his bicycle. He gripped the roughened iron handles so hard that by the time he reached the Place Saint-André-des-Arts the palms of his hands were bloody.

He stood outside the theatre, watching the crowd jostle one another through the doors. Above, on the marquee, in large reflecting letters illuminated by upward-turned lamps, were the words Le "Mermaid" de Paris. The audience entering the doors was well dressed, expectant, almost giddy. He found himself reluctant to push his way through and so waited for the lobby to clear and the usher to begin ringing his bell.

The ticket seller was counting a stack of bills behind the grill. "Excuse me, may I have one ticket please?"

"Sorry, we're sold out. Do you want a ticket for next week?"

"No, that's all right."

He backed away, relieved to have had the chance denied him. Outside again, he waited against the lamppost where he had left his bicycle. He waited as dusk turned to night and the electric street lights came on and the horse cabs grew less frequent. He could not control the trembling of his body.

A hard tap on his shin made him jump. A policeman stood beside him, swinging his stick, a short man in a new uniform with shining brass buttons. "You can't stand here all night," the policeman said. "Move on now."

Henry nodded without speaking and mounted his bicycle. He rode a block, circled round, and came back to the theatre. Again he waited, his agitation subsiding and then increasing again until finally the theatre doors were thrown open and the crowd poured out. They pushed past him in their rush to get cabs or find their own carriages. After the stragglers came out, the ushers pulled the doors closed again.

The marquee lights went out.

He was standing in the wrong place. How could he have been so stupid? Of course there would be a back door for the performers and musicians and stagehands to enter and leave. He must have missed them. But just as he turned to go around the back he saw them coming out from the alley. Belinsky, closer to him, blocked most of his view of Margaret as he led her by the arm to a waiting cab. She wore a velvet cape and a hat tilted forwards so that it shadowed her face from the street lamp, yet when he glimpsed her stepping into the cab he thought her face looked thin and pale. Belinsky saw her up and then bounded in after her, and the cab pulled away.

Henry scrambled onto his bicycle. Catching his trouser cuff in the chain, he tore it free and propelled himself into the street and the after-theatre traffic. He followed the cab, whose blinds had been lowered, up St. Martin and onto the Rue du 4 Septembre. Either the pedalling or the panic was exhausting him, for he was winded and gasping by the time they passed the opera house. He coasted a moment and was almost flattened by an omnibus, the driver jangling his bell. Henry pedalled on.

At the Place Vendôme the cab pulled up in front of the new Ritz Hotel. So as not to be seen, he rode past and made a wobbly circle back, pulling up behind a shut-up newspaper kiosk. Belinsky emerged first, turning and holding out his hand for her, then grasping her other arm as she came down the step. He directed her up the carpeted stairs as the doorman saluted them. Just as she was going through she half turned back and tried to see behind her, as if she knew he was there. But Belinsky was holding firmly to her arm and made her turn around again.

And they were inside and gone. He stood looking at where she had been, seeing through the glass doors to the glittering chandeliers, the enormous vases of roses, the pageboys crossing the carpet. He was not dreaming but awake. On his bicycle again, he rode steadily away.

He roused Emile from his potato-sack bed by the cellar coal bin. The hunchback tried to pull the covers over his head.

"Go away, Henri. My head is throbbing."

"Next time drink better absinthe. You must get up, Emile. I'll buy you a coffee and a roll on the way."

"Where do we have to go in such a hurry?"

"First the theatre and then the flea market."

"I've got enough fleas down here."

"If I didn't need your help, I wouldn't ask for it."

"All right, I can hear you're serious. See, I'm getting up. My God, the room is turning. Where are my trousers?"

"On your legs, where you left them. Here are your shoes."

Henry walked swiftly to the Théâtre Sous le Pont, carrying a bucket of paste in his hand, Emile trying to keep up. Emile said, "I don't get it. What gives?"

But Henry would not answer. At the theatre door, he pulled a rolled sheet of paper from his back pocket, ran the paste brush over the door, and pasted down the paper, running the brush over it.

Le
spectacle
est
terminé

"Cancelled? But why, Henri? We're making good money. For once in my life I don't have to choose between eating and drinking."

"Now to the market. We'll take a cab."

"At least tell me what is so important that you had to wake me up and spoil a very pleasant dream. What exactly are we going to buy?"

"Pistols."

"Lord Jesus, what for?"

"I need you to be my second. I found the man who stole my wife."

"Henri, this is the dawn of the twentieth century. Hardly anyone fights duels anymore. It's unseemly."

"I believe he is also the murderer of Giancarlo Caporale."

"You've never said so before. But even so, why a duel? They are an aristocratic affectation and against anarchist principles. Assassinations are a different matter, of course. We could simply—"

"It has to be a duel."

"I feel obliged to point out, Henri, the practical consideration of the law. It is very strict. Of course I understand that it's a matter of honour and so forth. But from a certain perspective, it really seems hardly worth the bother."

"If you don't wish to be my second I'll find someone else. Philippe, perhaps."

"The baker's assistant? He'll bungle the whole thing. Hold on, Henri, at least let me catch up."

Henry waved down an open cab and sat very still, hardly registering Emile's words as the hunchback continued his attempt to dissuade him. Finally giving up, Emile changed tactics. "All right, but if I'm to be your second, then you have to listen to my advice. There are rules, understand? If you don't conduct a duel according to the proper rules, then the whole thing is a sham. Tell me at least, are you a good shot?"

"I can't say."

"What do you mean, you can't say?"

"With a rifle and shotgun, yes. But I've never used a pistol so it's hard to judge."

"Oh this looks better and better, Henri. The odds are more in our favour every minute."

The streets around the market were clogged with wagons. Henry paid the cab and they made their way from one stall to another. The merchants shook their heads, insisting that no such guns were to be had at any price. Someone suggested trying the stall by the café, someone else the vendor across from the École de Musique. Then a stall just at the end of the rug sellers. And finally Monsieur Lefebvre at the fading end of the market.

Monsieur Lefebvre had not a stall but a shop that smelled of camphor and was so cluttered with chairs, trunks, musical instruments, and even wooden legs hanging from the ceiling that it would have been impossible to find anything. Monsieur Lefebvre himself was invisible until he stood up, an old but still large man, with a dirty yellow patch over one eye, sucking on an empty pipe.

"What is it you want?"

"Duelling pistols," Emile said. "We're looking for a matched set naturally."

"A good set of pistols is hard to come by these days. And not cheap. The police don't exactly encourage the selling of them and we've got our licences to think of."

"Have you got a pair?"

The merchant looked not at Emile but at Henry. He licked his dry bottom lip. "You ask if I have got a pair. If I do, it is no ordinary pair but something special. A work of art."

"As long as they fire," Emile said. "Show us."

A noisy clearing of phlegm from his throat. "With guns it's always hurry, hurry, as if the other fellow can't be permitted to live another three minutes. Wait a moment." He rose with difficulty and shuffled to a cabinet, taking a large ring of keys from his jacket. The drawer pulled out only with difficulty; he drew out a leather case, well rubbed at the corners but with handsomely worked hinges and clasp. He shuffled back and placed it on the desk.

"Feast your eyes, gentlemen." He unlatched the top and raised it.

"Mother of God, he isn't joking, Henri."

Henry looked at the twin guns nestled in their felt-lined recesses, the barrel of one almost touching the grip of the other. The barrels were of gleaming blue steel, etched in a delicate filigree of unfurling fronds, the design extending to the firing mechanism and the elegantly curving and highly polished mahogany stocks. Each cock was a sinuous silver *S* with a wedge of amber flint delicately clamped at the end. And in their various compartments the necessary accessories: mallet, pincers, powder flask, bullet mould, rod.

"They were made in the workshop of Nicholas Boutet. Late 1790s, I would say. Made for Alfred, the Duc d'Annecy, who was rather a hothead. Fought at least a dozen duels and was finally killed in the last. They were kept in the family until just this year. The usual money troubles. I've already had them cleaned. Go ahead, pick one up."

Henry did so, weighing it in the palms of his hands. Not as heavy as he expected. Perfectly balanced.

"Go ahead, try the trigger. It pulls like silk."

He shifted his grip. The stock was almost sensuous in his hand. He pulled back the cock. Raised the pan. Pointed into the shop and squeezed. A sharp snap and a little firework of sparks.

"Accurate within twenty paces only, on account of the smooth barrels. Treasures, they are. I couldn't let them go for less than two thousand francs."

"You are trying to insult us!" Emile said.

"It's all right," Henry said. He held the gun out again. Pulled back the cock. Snap.

"This is important, Henri. I want you to listen to me. First of all, position. You must stand sideways, with your shoulder towards your adversary, in order to lessen your size as a target. Stamp your feet a couple of times to set them firmly. Left arm hanging, stomach drawn in. Don't grasp the pistol too tightly; that will only make it tremble. When you raise it and aim, choose some small point such as the button of his coat. Fire without hesitation. Above all, you must remain calm and steady and think of nothing but hitting your object. Do not concern yourself with his gun at all. Do you hear me? Damn it, Henri, you're not paying the slightest attention."

"Why are you still here, Emile? Go and offer the challenge. Go now."

Waiting for Emile to return, he paced his room, craned his neck at the window to see if the hunchback might be coming into the courtyard, paced again. The pistol case lay on the bed but he did not touch it, nor the photograph album beside it. He could not find a single clear thought in his aching head; if only Emile would stop taking his time.

The sound of heavy footfalls on the stairs. He got to the door just as Emile came in, breathless after the climb.

"Well, did you make the challenge?"

"Give me a... chance... to catch my breath. It wasn't easy to find him, you know. Finally I bribed the doorman at the hotel to tell me that he goes to see his lawyer near the Bourse on Thursday mornings. You should have seen him, dressed in a frock coat like a regular businessman. Only he looks like a wrestler—"

"Get on with it, Emile. Was he surprised to hear from me?"

"I'll say. Here, let me sit down." He pulled from his pocket a square of rag, unravelling at the edges, and wiped his face. "I told him that I had a message from my friend Mr. Henri Cherche. You know what he answered? 'Who the devil is that?' I had to say your name the English way for him to understand. Ch-ur-ch. Damnably hard on the mouth. His eyes almost fell out of his bald head."

"And he accepted?"

"Once he started breathing again. He had no choice. After all, that Russian runt did steal your wife. He named his own second, some Leduc who works in the offices of the Lyric Theatre. I told him we had pistols and he agreed to use them. But he tried to intimidate us, Henry. He told me that he was an excellent shot and that since he had already survived two other challenges he would not be troubled by a third."

"I trust to my own skill."

"Yes, of course. I said as much. Oh, there is one thing. He did have one condition, and since he is the one being challenged I had no choice but to agree."

"What is that?"

"Perhaps you ought to sit down before I tell you."

"Stop delaying, Emile."

"He insists that the duel be held on bicycles."

"What? Bicycles? That is ridiculous. Is he trying to insult me?"

"I suggested that very thing. But he said that it was very common in Russia. He would have it no other way. I tell you, Henri, that smooth ape is not to be trusted. If I were you—"

"Enough, Emile. I have no doubt this is a condition of your own, insisted upon by you, to make it less likely that either of us will be hit or perhaps to give me an advantage. I will not have it."

"You're wrong, Henri, and I'm hurt that you would even suggest it. But it is already agreed on so there is nothing for it. He said he would bring his own bicycle. And a doctor, as is required by the rules of duelling."

"You told him that this is to remain secret, especially from the lady in question."

"Of course. He agreed. And this evening I will pay a call on his second to make the final arrangements."

"Very well. Just one last thing, then. How did Belinsky look when you left him?"

"In truth? He had an oddly pleased smile on his face. Really, Henri, you must kill the son of a bitch."

The raven flew in through the window, skittering across the table and causing Emile to almost fall out of his chair. "Satanic creature! It always scares the daylights out of me. Henri, we ought to practise. I suggest we use that bird as a target."

"I don't want to practise. If only I could speak to her—"

"Don't even think of it, Henri. I hope you know that a duel cannot win back a woman. It is for revenge only, a satisfaction that lasts a short time, I'm afraid."

"And when did you become so wise?"

"Hunchbacks are born wise, don't you know that? And we're lucky too, so it's a good thing I'm your second."

"Enough. I can't talk anymore, Emile. Please leave me alone."

He listened to the footsteps receding down the stairs. The bird cocked its head to look at him. He could do nothing but lie down on his bed, beside the guns and the album, and close his eyes.

She was reaching out to him through bars of pearl, her hand extended, fingers wanting only to reach and grasp his own. Her hair floated about her face and her eyes—so large and filled with love and hopelessness. Her mouth forming his name, calling him ...

He opened his eyes and saw Emile above him, gently shaking his shoulders and saying something he couldn't make out. The room was still dark. Was it time? To kill Belinsky in the duel would free her from servitude and debasement. To kill Belinsky would return her to him.

He rose from the bed. Splashed cold water on his face. "What are we waiting for, Emile? Let's go."

A mist clung to the base of the long stone wall and the trunks of the plane trees spaced widely in the clearing. The night chill had not yet lifted. He watched Emile get down from the cab first and handed him the case, wrapped in a blanket. He, too, got down, his foot half slipping from the iron step, and then they both untied the black bicycle from behind. The cab rattled away as the raven wheeled overhead. He wondered how they looked from up there, dark specks on a green expanse.

Holding the case under one arm, Emile lit a cheroot. "I still think this is a bad business, Henri. If you shoot him you will have to leave France or face arrest. And if he kills you, well, then you are quite dead."

"I seriously doubt either of us will do anything except cause a flat tire," Henri said, although he knew very well that he would kill Belinsky. "I don't understand how someone could have thought of such a thing as a duel on a bicycle. If I could have refused—"

"Belinsky insisted on it. Obviously, he is a peculiar man. As you know, I argued with his second, that Leduc, but it did no good. Come, let's wait farther into the clearing. It's very bad form of them to be late."

They walked on, Henry wheeling the bicycle and Emile hoisting the blanket-wrapped case under his arm. The grass was uncut and the dew soaked the bottom of their trouser legs. As they waited, the sky lightened and the mist began to dissipate. Emile shifted the case to his other arm.

"It wouldn't do to have the damn powder get wet. Maybe the famous strongman has decided to sneak out of Paris with his tail between his legs. It wouldn't surprise me to discover he is a coward without a single—ah, there he is at last."

Three figures had appeared in the distance, with no carriage in sight. He could easily make out the bowlegged count as the one in the middle. As they neared he could guess that Leduc was the one pushing the bicycle, while the doctor, the tallest, wore a silk hat.

"Wait here, Henri. I'll talk to them first. You and Belinsky must not exchange words."

Still with the case under his arm, Emile advanced towards the men as they approached. They met beneath a plane tree, the count hanging back to let the other two men confer with Emile. Henry could hear the sound of their voices but not what they said. Emile laid the blanket on the ground, the case on top of it. He opened the case. Leduc chose a pistol and Emile picked up the other. After more conferring, the seconds each in turn measured and then poured the powder into the barrels, wrapped the lead balls in squares of cloth, and pushed them down with the rod. After this came gestures towards the clearing, heads shaking, voices rising in disagreement. At last there were nods and handshakes and the doctor, who was carrying a bag, retreated some twenty yards.

Emile carried the pistol into the clearing. "Monsieur Cherche," he called out. "Would you please come with your bicycle and take up your mark." And so, it would really happen, just as he had imagined. As he started forwards he felt a weakness in one knee, as if his leg had been drained of blood. But he kept going, rolling the bicycle over the uneven grass. He could smell the damp and hear, in the distance, an axe chopping wood. The sun was now hazy, burning off the remains of the mist.

He reached Emile and turned his bicycle in the direction of the count at the other end of the clearing. Emile said, "All right, Henri. Mount your bicycle and I'll hand you the pistol. Hold it properly now. Don't forget to calculate a slight drop in the ball's arc if you shoot from any distance. But I think you ought to get close—only, whatever you do, don't wait for him to get off the first shot. Now, when Leduc drops his handkerchief the two of you are to ride towards one another. You may fire at will. The Russian is shaking like a leaf. He's going to get what he deserves and he knows it. So go ahead, Henri. Take your vengeance."

As Emile walked away he made the sign of the cross. He went to stand beside Leduc, who already had a yellow handkerchief in his hand. For some reason, Henry felt annoyed by the colour. He looked at Belinsky, who was on his own gleaming bicycle, obviously new, the pistol raised, its barrel glinting in the low sun. The yellow handkerchief went up. Henry positioned himself over the horizontal bar, one foot on the ground, the other on a pedal. He tipped his own gun upwards. Leduc took a step forwards.

"Ready!" Leduc shouted.

The handkerchief dropped.

He had some trouble starting; the front wheel dipped into an indentation in the ground, tipping him to one side. But he pushed hard on the pedals, almost losing hold of the pistol but giving the bicycle the necessary momentum. Now he managed to raise the pistol and turn his eyes towards Belinsky, who was approaching more slowly. Suddenly they seemed much closer to each other. He could see the grim look on Belinsky's red face, muscles straining as his bicycle moved unevenly over the ground. His gun, too, pointed forwards, the mouth of the barrel a small black hole. But then Belinsky raised his gun over his head, the bicycle weaving even more, and pointing it in the air, fired. Henry saw the flash and heard the crack but he kept pedalling, as did Belinsky, so that they were just three bicycle lengths away, then almost beside one another. He did not want mercy and would not offer it, and he pointed his gun at the middle of the count's chest and squeezed the trigger hard and there was a brilliant light and roar and a searing heat in his own hand. The bicycle slid out from beneath him and his back hit the ground and he was trembling furiously and could smell only the nauseating odour of burning flesh.

Margaret—

The clouds scudding so quickly overhead.

For you— —

SUMMER 1902

A brilliant green scum had formed on the river, and a foul odour hung over the village. The low buildings, all made of the same whitish stone, looked to him as if they had arisen out of the earth. The Lion d'Or, the chemist's, the blacksmith's. By the church the flat tombstones, tilted and cracked, were of the same stone, as if to signify that the living and dead inhabited the same house. In front of the café were grouped a few wicker chairs, one of which was occupied by a sleeping cat. At the low end of the village the mill was silent, the water having fallen too low. From up the slope came the sound of a rug being beaten.

He had walked from the farm to the village, as he did every morning, past the fields of lavender and sunflowers. Along the way he had raised his limp hat to a pair of nuns and then a man leading a donkey. The man's French was difficult for Henry to understand. At the edge of the village several boys had followed him from a distance, running from one hiding place to the next.

This morning he decided not to turn right back but instead to enter the café. In the gloom of the interior he went up to the bar. Arget, the owner, was wiping glasses.

"A pastis, if you please."

The man took down the bottle, calling something to his wife in the kitchen. He poured the yellow liquid into a glass and added water before taking Henry's coin from the top of the bar. The remaining bandage on Henry's right hand meant he had to pick up the glass with his left, an awkwardness he still wasn't used to. He took his notebook from his jacket pocket but did not open it. He hadn't opened it all these weeks but found some comfort in its presence.

Outside again, he squinted in the light. The chemist, sweeping before his shop, paused to wave. The man had changed Henry's bandage several times and was the only person to go out of his way to speak to him, as if to show the others his bravery or sophistication. Henry waved back and walked back through the village and down the road. Once more he was enveloped in the perfume of the lavender fields. The raven appeared in the sky as a black speck, grew larger, and landed in the dust of the road. It waddled along with him for a minute or two before throwing itself up into the air again. Soon Henry could see the farmhouse's broken chimney. Approaching it, he passed various debris; a broken wagon wheel, a disintegrating wine cask, a rusting hoe.

As it was a pleasant day, the father had been untied from his bed and chained by the ankle to the cypress tree in front of the house. The chain was perhaps ten feet long, allowing for some movement but preventing his running away or climbing the roof of the house to crow like a rooster. The father would not allow anyone to touch his beard, and it now reached down to his waist.

Seeing Henry come up the dirt path, the man said, "I am bringing my beloved marble sofa to the dance on Friday."

"May I sit with you, old Father?"

Henry took the other wooden chair under the tree. He spent most mornings keeping company with a man who had lost his mind ten years before, on the death of his wife. The raven dived low, frightening the goats in the pen, and rose again to caw from the roof in imitation of the local crows.

The old man said, "If only the birds would stop lifting

the women's dresses." Henry closed his eyes and felt the warm sun on his face.

Even with his bandaged hand, Henry insisted on helping Clothilde with the washing. She filled the barrel with water and soap and sheets while he put on the lid and turned the crank with much effort. Afterwards he fed them through the wringer and she hung them up on the line.

Clothilde started late in the kitchen and it was well after dark when he sat with her father and three brothers at the long table in the front room for supper. Hunger kept the three brothers from saying a word during the soup course, during which they soaked their thick slices of bread in the broth and let it drip down their chins as they ate.

Clothilde brought in a dish of boiled spinach and another of beets. The middle brother said, "I hear that Guillaume has bought up Pascal's land."

"Then he'll have the biggest vineyard around here, won't he?" said the youngest. "We'll have to work for him in the harvest. And he's a real skinflint."

The eldest gulped the remains of his second glass of wine. "I suppose in a primitive country like Canada the men do the women's work. Washing, cooking, making the beds."

Clothilde, bringing in the veal, said, "Don't start again, Maurice."

"I don't understand how a person can be such an imbecile. Buying a gun with a fracture in the firing mechanism. Even worse, losing your hand over a woman."

"Not the whole hand," Henry said mildly. "Two and a half fingers."

"But what are you good for now, eh? Not even this—"

He made an obscene gesture. Clothilde said, "I won't have disgusting talk at the supper table."

"But Maurice is right," said the middle brother. "Here he eats our food, takes up one of our rooms. And who is going to take you off our hands, Clothilde, while he's hanging about? We can't expect any sort of good match."

Clothilde picked up a serving knife and pointed it towards her middle brother's throat. "And who are you to talk?" she cried. "The only girl you had the nerve to ask to marry you laughed in your face and took the butcher instead. Henri here almost died for love, while you—" she turned her knife on the oldest brother—"for you it's enough to satisfy yourself with the goats. And even they don't like you."

The brother began to rise. "I won't take that," he began, but Henry rose too and gently removed the knife from Clothilde's hand.

"Clothilde, why don't you sit down and eat for once. I'll serve."

"No, I prefer to eat in the kitchen. It's no wonder I ran away to Paris. And if we hadn't needed somewhere to go they would never have heard from me again."

She banged the kitchen door shut as she retreated. The brothers resumed their eating.

"You shouldn't get her so riled up," the youngest brother said, clutching his knife and fork in his fists. "Or else we'll be eating Maurice's vile cooking again."

"Even fish deserve a republican government," said their father, his mouth red from the beets.

He had a small room at the back of the farmhouse, with an iron bedstead, a table, a square of old sacking over the window. He sat on the edge of the bed, working the tip of a kitchen knife underneath the bandage wrapped round his hand. A knock sounded on the door.

"Henri?"

Clothilde entered, her hands red from washing up, her hair in disarray. "What are you doing?"

"Taking this thing off."

"But shouldn't you let the chemist do it?"

"Ouch, I pricked myself." He stopped and looked up at her. "Perhaps you shouldn't watch this, Clothilde."

She crossed her arms, her face taking on its stubborn look. "Who was it that took care of you on the way from Paris? Go on. If you're going to do it get it over with."

He resumed sawing at the bandage. The knife went through the last threads and he put it down and pulled the two sides apart. The skin beneath was sensitive to touch. The wound had healed fairly cleanly, but his hand had been turned into a claw. The first two fingers were missing and the first joint of the third. The skin was a hatchwork of scars. He tried to move the thumb towards the remaining fingers.

Clothilde came down onto the bed beside him. "Does it hurt?"

"Not very much anymore. The chemist says you did a good job taking care of it at the beginning, which was the crucial time. Otherwise it would have become infected. I haven't deserved this kindness from you, Clothilde."

"I don't think what we get has anything to do with what we deserve. And I am tired of your thanks. Now," she said as she rose, "I'm going to read the new issue of *Le Libertaire* until I fall asleep. I'm always exhausted on laundry day."

He reached up to grasp her arm with his good hand. "Clothilde, stay."

Gently she pulled away. "Goodnight, Henri. Dream of something new for a change. Like an invention that will take me away from here."

He was sitting under the cypress tree with the father when a horse and cart came up the dirt road. The figure beside the driver looked familiar but not until it grew closer could he make out that distinctive head and the hunched shoulders.

"Emile!" He stood up and waved, while the raven shrieked from a fence post. The cart came to a halt and Emile jumped nimbly down, pulling an overstuffed sack after him. Henry strode up and the two embraced.

"Why didn't you send a message that you were coming?"

"I wanted to, but Armand said it would be risky. The police have got it into their heads to make a big show of throwing us all in jail. We've all had to find new digs. Anyway, I can't even stay the night. I'm on my way to a meeting in Toulouse. Finding this out-of-the-way hole has taken too much time as it is. Come, let's sit down. I picked up a couple of bottles in the village."

They sat under the cypress and shared the wine with the father. "It's a shame that Clothilde is at the market today, selling goat cheese," Henri said. "She'll be sorry she missed you."

"Oh, not so sorry. I could never get anywhere with that one. Tell me, are her brothers as savage as she described?"

"A little worse, I'm sorry to say. So tell me, how is Armand?"

"The same as always. When things get more difficult, he just takes it as a sign that we are closer to changing the world. Here, old one," he said to the father, "your glass is empty."

"Rubbing a hunchback will grow hair on a bald man," the father said.

"See, Henri? I'm good for many things."

They remained silent a moment. Henry said, "Have you found out anything more?"

"A little. As I suspected, Belinsky went back to Russia to avoid arrest."

"And Margaret did not go with him?"

"It does not seem so. She just disappeared, even leaving her luggage behind. Perhaps she went back to Canada."

"Perhaps."

"It's the end of that story, Henri. Time to start a new one."

Each of them took a long drink of wine. The branches of the cypress tree made barred shadows across their legs.

❧

She had the palest freckles on her eyelids, above her lip, on the lobes of her ears. Deepening on her small breasts, her belly, her thighs—a random pattern, as if they had been strewn upon her while she slept. He kissed here there. And there. And there.

She murmured, "What are you doing? It's late."

"I want to know you, Clothilde."

He moved down her body while she entwined her fingers in his hair, giving off soft sounds. He reached the tender slope to her sex. Taste of pungent honey. She stirred under him and began to moan quietly. The moans became cries and the cries louder as she pulled on his hair, then wild humming and fragmented utterances, so that one of the brothers started pounding on the wall. She came out of her trancelike state long enough to call out, "You shut up!"

She pulled him up, and he felt her flat pelvis slide beneath him. He slipped inside her, arching upwards, unable to stop himself, calling her name. He lowered himself to kiss her mouth.

They held each other. She tried to speak. He felt her hot tears.

Taking the goats to better pasture, the brothers threw stones at the raven, which flew to a higher perch and shat, hitting the rim of the eldest brother's grimy felt hat. Clothilde had already milked the goats to begin the day's cheese-making, and she did not want Henry's help until it was time to strain and hang the cheese. So he began his walk to town, taking the longer route past Guillaume's vineyards, where the vines sagged with the maturing grapes, dusty in the sun. He reached the village and went to the chemist's shop, which was also the village post office, and up to Monsieur Gerard, who was wearing his pristine white jacket as always and vigorously grinding away with mortar and pestle.

"Ah, Monsieur Ch-ur-ch," he said, attempting the English pronunciation, "you are up early."

"Monsieur Gerard, if I might have a sheet of paper, an envelope, and postage for Canada, I would be obliged to you."

"One moment, monsieur. Let me just finish this powder for Madame Lavoie. Digestive troubles, you know." He spoke confidentially, wagging his sharp little beard. Clothilde had told Henry that the chemist was detested by all the women of the village, who were forced to reveal to him their secrets. The man poured the powder into an envelope taken from one of the little wooden drawers behind the counter, sealed it, and wrote out the label in a precise hand. Then he gave Henry the paper and envelope. "Just return it to me when you're done, and I'll affix the postage."

A writing desk stood in the corner of the shop. Henry laid down the sheet and picked up the pen, dipping the steel nib into the bottle of ink. Writing with his left hand was slow and laborious work.

Neuilluey-en-Rive
September 24, 1902

Dear Chester,

Much time has passed since you last heard from me, or rather saw me in your office in a rather agitated state. I am convalescing in the countryside after having suffered a minor injury in an accident. Some lost fingers are the reason for the poor penmanship. I have some interesting ideas that I wish to follow up but require my last two notebooks, which you may recall I left in your possession. Would you send them to the above address, along with Lilienthal's Bird Flight as the Basis of Aviation *and Chanute's* Progress of Flying Machines, *care of the postmaster.*

Yours faithfully,
Henry Church

P.S. Any word about the condition of my father-in-law, Jeremiah Dawes, would be appreciated.

He had smudged the ink with the side of his hand in several places. He blew on it to dry it and then folded the paper and placed it into the envelope. Two days ago he had started writing in his notebook again, a sudden flurry of ideas. It felt as if his mind had woken up after a long, numbing slumber. The chemist smiled at Henri as he licked the stamp himself and placed it on the envelope, smoothing it with his thumb.

Straddling him, she let her hair fall over his face and chest. Her face above him as she looked into his eyes and then brought her mouth to his. The rope bed sang beneath them.

"See, Henri. I am fucking you back to health."

The landowner Guillaume reluctantly took on Henry for the grape harvest, only because, what with buying Pascal's vineyards as well and two sons run off to Marseilles, he did not have enough workers. "Even a man with one and a half hands is better than nothing," he said, and besides, he paid by the basket, so it didn't matter if Henry was slower than the others.

The fall sun was hot, the work exhausting. His left hand grew cramped from cutting the stalks and his back quickly began to ache. The raven hopped about him for the first two days, feasting on crickets, then decided to remain on the farm in the company of the mad father. How could he have imagined ending up here, loading his basket with heavy grapes, listening to the men singing? He wanted to believe that there was some reason for it, and he suspected now that beneath his scientific outlook there had long been something more vague but also perhaps more powerful, a secret desire for faith. It had emerged only in his love for Margaret. She had become his religion, he could see that now, and in losing her he had been suddenly deprived of all that sustained him. He had believed himself incapable of living without her. Yet here he was, with a mangled hand, picking grapes in a French field, assured that Clothilde would be waiting for him back at the farm. He could think. He could make love. So he was alive after all. Without faith but alive.

Guillaume's remaining son called the lunch break. Men became visible among the rows as they stood up and stretched. He cut one more bunch of grapes and put it in the basket. How good a tin cup of water would taste.

It took seven weeks for the package to arrive from Canada. "The French postal system is the best in the world," said the chemist, placing it on the counter. "Would you like me to open it for you?"

"That is very kind of you, but no, I will take it with me. Good day."

He carried the package under his arm back to the farm. The lavender fields had turned brown. The row of apple trees along the vineyard roads had fruit rotting beneath them. Only when he was seated beside the old man under the cypress tree did he cut the strings and pull away the stiff paper. Tucked inside one of the notebooks was a letter.

Dear Henry,

Are you absolutely mad? The last time we met you were about to embark on a misguided chase for your wife. Since then I have not had a single word from you. And now you turn up in some place too small to appear on a map and report that you have misplaced several fingers? I'm surprised you did not comment on the weather.

As you requested, I send your notebooks. I had thought that you had put aside the problem of aerial locomotion. The British, the Germans, the Americans, and everyone else is racing to build the first true flying machine. If I were you, I would stick to bicycles. However, I include the books as well as the most recent articles. I wish you luck and suggest that you take care not to misplace any more parts of yourself.

Your bewildered friend,
Chester

P.S. On a solemn note, I must report that your father-in-law, Jeremiah Dawes, passed away from natural causes some two months after your departure. His funeral was, according to his own wishes, private. This was reported in the newspapers. Before his death he arranged for the sale of the bicycle company to CCM. The price he received (apparently much reduced) has been placed in trust for Margaret should she ever return. If not, it will eventually be given to the orphanage where you spent your childhood.

Henry sat for some time with the loose package in his lap. The father whittled at a hickory stick with a spoon, as it was unwise to allow him a knife. The raven, who seemed fond of the old man, walked around the chairs, bobbing its head and making sounds like Morse code. So his benefactor was dead, the man who had lifted Henry from poverty into respectability, had agreed to the marriage of his daughter, had tried to build a solid edifice to safeguard those most closely allied to him. And all of it had crumbled.

The old father said, "There is nothing more lamentable in this world, my son, than the pain of a broken harpsichord."

The errors in his own drawings were much clearer to him now. For one thing, the tail assembly, which was far less stable than Pained's. For another the wings. They were too short; Wenham's paper to the Aeronautical Society proved that longer wings provided more lift. There was something to learn from the Henson-Stringfellow model as well.

He worked at the uneven table by the whitewashed wall in the bedroom. Even with the addition of the modifications, his vision was his own. Chester had advised him to stick with bicycles; well, he had. His design was no less than a bicycle that could fly, a machine powered by its human rider. Man-powered flight had been discarded by the others, who were building lighter steam engines or engines using the new combustion method. But a proper chain and gear assembly might just allow a man pedalling to turn a propeller with enough speed to create the necessary thrust. If the machine itself was light enough. True, he was having trouble getting the mathematics to work out, but he had always been an instinctive inventor anyway.

A noise outside made him look up. Clothilde's brothers, coming home drunk again. They would soon be snoring in their beds. He couldn't much blame their resentment of him, but he hoped it wouldn't prevent them from aiding him in gathering some of the materials he needed. A light flexible wood for the frame and unsized cotton to cover the wing struts. The chain workings of two good bicycles. He himself would assemble it all and carve the propeller if he could borrow some tools.

He heard the door open. Clothilde entered, carrying two small glasses of white liqueur.

"Here, Henri, drink this. The monks make it down in the valley."

He stood up to take the glass, gave her the smile of approval she needed, and drank it down. She looked down at his notebook on the desk. "Why do you insist on working on that? First it was the puppet show and now this. I'm no inventor, but I don't see how that contraption will rise up in the air."

"Well, it can't exactly. It would be impossible to pedal fast enough to create the necessary lift. I'll have to launch it from some high point. With the air under its wings, I think the power will be enough to keep it aloft for several minutes."

She put her arms around his neck and he kissed her. "But why do you have to build it at all? I don't see how that's going to help us get off this farm."

"I don't suppose I'm thinking about why, Clothilde. I'm just doing it."

"Well, I'm thinking about it. You want to fly away from me."

"No. But perhaps I want to fly away from myself. In a way, I do when I'm just thinking about it."

"Henri, women come from all over to buy the monk's liqueur. It's supposed to make the man who drinks it fall in love with you."

He looked into her eyes. "What would your anarchist friends say about that?"

He began to unbutton her dress and kiss her between her breasts. She pulled him closer and took his hand to press it between her legs.

"You'll never love me," she murmured.

"Shh."

"It'll always be that woman who made you so miserable. You keep those photographs of her—I look at them. Sometimes I feel like she's watching us."

"She isn't. You're an angel sent, don't you know that?"

"Then I'm an angel with a temper. You know what I'm going to do? Where are those photographs?"

"Clothilde—"

She broke away from him and snatched the album up from the foot of the bed. Without saying a word she ran from the room, clutching it in her arms. He didn't follow, but waited for her to return. And she did, almost as if she had just stepped out the door and come right back, her eyes shining with glee.

"There! I threw it into the fire. You should have seen how quickly it flared up. It made very pretty colours." She stepped towards him. "Are you angry with me?"

"No. It's just as well." And it was true; he didn't need them to remember her. He put his arm around Clothilde's waist and brought her to the bed.

The youngest brother helped him find the materials and build the frame, perhaps to defy his brothers, perhaps because his curiosity had not been totally extinguished. He had managed to find two rusted bicycles in the next village, and from these they had made the pedal-and-chain system and the wheel assembly with the assistance of the blacksmith, who had welded eyeholes onto them so that they could be screwed into the larger wooden structure.

They spent a day tacking the cloth onto the wings, the only elegant part of the machine. By the end of the day his claw hand was throbbing. When they came in, the others were already sitting at the dinner table waiting to be served. As Clothilde came in, the eldest brother said, "This man she brought is so mad he might as well be English."

The middle brother said, "And what will he do with a flying bicycle, eh? Take the mail to Rouen?"

The father began spooning up the soup immediately after his bowl was filled. Without looking up, he said, "That bird is an angel in disguise. Anyone with eyes can see that."

"It isn't an angel, it's a rat with feathers," said the eldest brother. "But I'll say one thing for it, at least it can fly. That piece of junk in the front yard certainly won't. You know what I call it? A coffin with wings."

Henry watched Clothilde's face go white. "Go wash your ugly face, Maurice," she said. "Otherwise there's no supper for you."

As they lay end to end, he caressed her narrow foot, running his finger along the sole, outlining her funnily shaped little toe.

"Maybe my brother is right," she said. "Maybe you are building your own coffin."

"I don't think so, Clothilde."

"Think?" She rolled over, pulling her foot from his hand. "You aren't sure? That's very comforting, Henri. Since you started building that thing you do almost nothing else. And what happens when you are finished? You don't have to tell me, I already know. You are going to leave."

He hadn't quite faced the truth of that himself, but hearing her, he knew that she was right. He wanted to say that he wouldn't leave, or leave without her, but he couldn't get the words out. So he turned on his side towards her and began to kiss her thigh. He moved up, but she kept her legs tightly together.

"As an anarchist, I did not believe in God," she said. "Now maybe I think that there really is a God and that he enjoys playing terrible jokes on us."

"Perhaps you're right."

Her thighs eased. "Ah, that's nice, Henri. Please go on."

The envelope handed to him by Monsieur Gerard, the chemist, was from Emile, back in Paris. There was no letter, just an article cut out of a Paris newspaper.

PEASANTS TAKE VENGEANCE

Another Sign of Increasing Instability in Russia

Disgruntled peasants in a district not far from the Russian city of Moscow took vengeance on their employer last month in an act seen as yet another sign that the society of Czar Nicholas is becoming increasingly unstable.

A group of peasants, hired to work in the fields, turned their scythes upon their employer, Count Anatole Belinsky, and

murdered him. According to reports, the killing was in retalia-
tion for some act of the Count's that angered the peasants,
ancestors of serfs who had been owned by the Belinsky family
before emancipation. The Czar has publicly denounced the mur-
der but has also called on landowners to treat the people with
dignity and fairness. Russian police have questioned all peas-
ants living on the late Count's estate but have made no arrests.

He read it just once before folding it up small and, after
purchasing a small box of matches from the chemist, taking
it into the street and letting it burn in the palm of his hand.

The aerial-cycle had been dismantled into three parts and
loaded into the back of a low ox cart. He tried to find
Clothilde to say goodbye, but she was nowhere in the
house, nor the barn, nor with the goats in the field. He
stood under the cypress tree and called out her name, but
still she didn't answer.

The three brothers, however, stood to watch him go,
while the driver of the ox cart waited for him to climb up.
The eldest brother personally threw Henry's travelling bag
into the back, "To make sure you don't change your mind."

Henry took the cage and approached the raven, which
was cleaning itself beside the father's split boots. The raven
fluttered up into the cypress tree and called down furiously.

"The bird won't go. Not until the world has been
cleansed of suffering."

"Or you stop feeding it, Father," Henry said. But he
would leave the bird; perhaps it did feel a greater sympathy
for the old man.

Henry pulled himself up onto the cart and the driver used his switch on the oxen's flank. The youngest brother called out, "I was glad to know you, Henri."

The cart rattled along the path. He felt a tightening in his chest, a yearning not for what lay ahead but for what he was leaving behind. He examined the sensation almost as if he were being given access to someone else's pain. It would take at least three days to reach the coast. The fall season was advanced, the winds more unpredictable now, but he did not want to wait out the winter. Then it would have been even harder to leave Clothilde. He had stayed in Paris to look for Margaret; he had remained on the farm to recover. There was no longer a reason to stay here. He could travel to the ends of the earth if he cared to.

FALL 1903

*T*he stone house did not appear to rest so much as balance on its promontory of rock. It looked to Henry as if a strong wind might shoulder it over the edge and into the waves below. The windows and doors were boarded up, but it took only an iron pole, found among the rubbish behind the house, to pry open the door. Light filtered in, illuminating the dust. Crumbling inner walls and a cold stone floor. A few broken pieces of furniture, a mattress inhabited by mice. The iron stove appeared sound, and a few pots and utensils had been left in the sagging cupboard. Standing in the house, he could hear the sea below, as if the house were a conch shell put to the ear.

He started by taking the boards from the windows, then sweeping with a broken-handled broom. He half-carried, half-pushed the parts of the aerial-cycle into the main room. He gathered wood for the stove.

The first night, he slept on his overcoat.

He was using a homemade ladder, applying mud between the stones of the north side of the house, when he saw a man approaching. As the man got nearer, Henry saw that he had a shotgun on his shoulder.

Henry waited on the ladder. The man stopped some ten paces short and touched his hat. "Fixing the house, are you?"

"Yes."

"What's your name?"

"Henry Church."

"Mine's Lavigne. You been here long?"

"Just arrived, actually."

"Planning to stay?"

"For a while."

The man rested the butt of the rifle on the ground. "Well, I must say it's kind of you to fix up my late uncle's house, which he left in his will to me."

"It didn't seem as if anyone had need of it for the moment."

"Not been lived in for eight or ten years. People have been known to turn crazy in that house is the reason. Nobody wants it. Still, it is my property."

"I don't have money to pay rent. But if you let me stay a while I'll do some repairs. And whenever you want it back you can have it."

"You'll fix the roof?"

"Certainly."

The man looked at Henry and spat into the coarse grass. "Where you from, with that accent?"

"Canada."

"You don't say. I might have some spare things that you could use. But remember, it's not my fault if you lose your mind like everyone else who's lived in it."

"Thank you for the warning."

The man nodded and walked away. Henry scooped more mud from the tin can.

He took an early morning walk along the cliff line and followed its gradual descent over some two miles down to the stony shore, where he found Lavigne working on his nets along with the other fishermen.

"Hey, monsieur," he called, "you want to go out with me? You can see what real work is like."

"I wouldn't accept if I were you," one of the other fishermen said, winking at the others. "Lavigne is famous for having three boats sink under him in the last twenty years."

"It was only two, and bad luck. I've got two bottles of wine to make the day more pleasant. Are you coming?"

"Yes, I'll come," Henry said.

He helped to haul the nets onto the boat, wading into the cold water in a pair of rubber boots that Lavigne had loaned him. They went out far enough for the shore to vanish, but the day was calm and the other boats could be seen gently rising and falling around them. Lavigne opened the first bottle of wine after the nets were out, and they passed it back and forth.

"I suppose you've pulled some interesting things out of the water with your nets," Henry said.

"That's true enough. A real knight's broadsword once, as had diamonds and rubies and such in its handle, only they'd rusted out. Another time a boot with a foot still in it. Turned out I knew the fellow it belonged to, though the boot wasn't much use to him anymore. And once a serpent with three heads."

"Yes?" said Henry.

"Maybe you don't believe me, but it's true. I was alone at sea as a storm was coming in. The fish were running and I didn't want to give up yet. But I said to myself, this is the last haul, only I had a hell of a time bringing it up, with whatever I'd caught thrashing something awful. It was an ugly thing, and as it broke the surface it spat and cursed with all three heads. It was all I could do to cut it free of my nets. I suppose if I'd brought it in I would have made my fortune, but I was scared out of my wits, and besides, a thing like that ought to go back to where it belongs. Of course, I've been considered a little touched ever since I told about it, but I won't ever take it back because I know what I saw. There are all kinds of creatures we know nothing of. Most people just don't want to believe it, and I suppose they don't have to."

Henry watched Lavigne finish the first bottle of wine and throw it into the bottom of the boat. "My daughters will meet us when we come in. Can you imagine, five children and not one boy to come to sea with me. Well, they'll be fishermen's, wives which is as bad or worse. I've told them about that hand of yours there, and they're terrified to see it. You might as well come for supper and give them a good scare."

Henry didn't answer. He would help unload the catch and then politely decline the invitation. It was time he set about doing what he had come here for.

The trip in the cart had caused some minor damage to the aerial-cycle: a tire gone flat, three small rips in the cotton stretched over the wings, dust clogging the chain. He spent the day methodically putting the machine to rights, repairing and pumping up the tire, sewing the rips, removing, soaking, and re-oiling the chain. Before dark he moved the separate parts onto the slope beside the house to assemble them. Then he stepped back to take in the impressive sight. The wings, set just above and behind the pilot's head, stretched nine feet in either direction. The body of the machine was twelve feet in length, including the stabilizing tail structure.

The pedals of the machine powered the propeller, not the wheels, which meant that only his initial push and gravity would provide the momentum down the slope to the cliff. He had to count on the air under the wings to keep the plane aloft for the few seconds it would take his pedalling speed to increase the propeller's rotation enough to provide the necessary thrust. A wind would help lift the aerial-cycle higher, but even without the wind it ought to glide for a good hundred yards before coming gently down onto the water.

He stayed there even as night fell and the aerial-cycle became an outline in the dark. And if it actually flew? He could not imagine his life after that moment.

He lay on the straw mattress provided by Lavigne, listening to the sea. And the wind too, swirling about the house, filling the emptiness. A man could not be more alone. He turned over, tried to will himself to sleep.

At dawn he stood by the window, scanning the moderately choppy sea. A dark speck bobbed halfway to the horizon. Or was he imagining it? No, there was nothing. His heart beat quickly, and he said to himself, *Calm, calm.*

The morning was like the first day of the world. The sky a whitish haze, as if new-formed, and the sea beneath not sparkling but bright and untouched. He slipped on his gloves and goggles and hauled the aerial-cycle by the tail to the top of the slope and pointed it down to the cliff. Without an assistant, he would have to push it himself until the machine began to roll from its own weight, when he would jump in and have to buckle the strap even as he began to pedal. He stood, took three deep breaths, and was about to start, when suddenly he remembered and ran back to the house.

The narrow box was on the floor beside the bed. He opened it and held the black pearls in his gloved hands a moment before bowing his head and placing the strand around his neck. He left the house and made his way back to the aerial-cycle. He set his feet firmly, counted aloud to three, and began to push. The machine moved sluggishly at first, but reluctantly began to pick up speed, the wings rattling. It began to move rapidly as the slope dipped, and he feared stumbling and letting go of the machine, watching it pass over the cliff without him. He threw himself in, struggling to get his feet on the pedals. Where was the other end of the belt? Caught somewhere beneath him— he would have to do without it. The cliff edge roared towards him, the sky growing larger, and then the machine hurled into the air—

And dived. The sea coming up towards him. As the machine plunged, the goggles pressing to his face, he clenched his body, hands pressed against their wooden supports. The impact of the water was a giant's slap against his body, ripping the goggles from his eyes. He was *in* the water, cold, sinking downwards, pieces of wing turning beside him and his own body rising out of the seat. He let out some air from his mouth and felt his foot catch on something— the belt he had not been able to find. He tried to kick free, but the weight of the machine kept pulling him downwards. He inhaled, and the cold and salt-bitter water entered his throat, stabbing his lungs. He began to thrash his arms, a more terrible pain penetrating his right lung. He felt violent spasms shake him, even as the light began to fade.

But the dark grew light again, iridescent. And there was Margaret, hovering before him, her beautiful face smiling just a little and her hair wavering like seaweed. He saw her mouth move, but could hear no words. She moved closer and pressed her lips to his, her mouth opening, and he felt the pain recede from his lungs. She pulled away a little to look at him, eyes brimming with sorrow. She took him in her arms and cradling him she moved upwards like a dove in the air.

When he awoke, the sun was low in the window. He lay on his bed, naked, legs tucked up to his chest, a pillow beneath his head. For a moment he did not move but just lay blinking and feeling the soreness of his body.

He turned over and looked about the room. Chair, rug, dresser—all the same. He got up slowly and found a shirt and a pair of trousers to put on before walking barefooted out the door. In the air around the house swallows dipped, catching insects. The patches of grass, the cliff edge, the distant sea—all the same.

He walked in measured steps to the cliff and looked below, but saw only water. So he followed the edge, continuing as it began to slowly descend. At his slow pace it took nearly an hour to reach the stony beach. It was deserted. He watched the waves roll up and wash back, revealing the smooth stones.

Looking out, he saw her.

She was not far, on a rock rising out of the water some twenty yards out. She was looking back at him, her hand shading her eyes, her hair fallen loose to her shoulders and breasts. The first line of scales began just below her navel; in colour they were so like her skin as to be almost indiscernible but for their sheen. Gradually they deepened to a speckled alternation of green and brownish gold, darkening to violet-black at the base of her tail before it widened into the fluke. She waved the fluke back and forth—it looked both firm and muscular—and then lowered it, slapping it against the rock. Only as he looked up to her face again did he notice the string of black pearls around her neck. If he had known, if he had only known. But perhaps he really had for the longest time. He took a step into the water, the cold pinpricks to his feet. He would plunge forwards, would swim until he reached the rock, and then he would be with her at last. But something in her look made him hesitate. She put a finger to her lips. Then she slipped into the water, tail first, and was gone

He stared at the rock, and the sea stretching infinitely behind it. All was still. He turned around and waded back onto the beach. He kept walking, the land rising away from the sea, and although he wanted to, he did not let himself look back.

AUTHOR'S NOTE

Some readers may hear echoes of other works in this novel, from Turgenev to Doctorow, from Flaubert to Marquez. I freely acknowledge the influence of my betters.

I wish to thank Joanne Schwartz, Bernard Kelly, and Jennifer Barclay for reading the manuscript and providing needed encouragement, as well as Anna Porter and Susan Renouf for their valuable suggestions. The Ontario Arts Council and the Toronto Arts Council provided financial support.